moon chilled

Moon Chilled
By Caitlin Ricci

Published by Less Than Three Press LLC

Edited by Amanda Jean
Cover designed by Aisha Akeju

Print Edition April 2014
Copyright © 2014 by Caitlin Ricci
Printed in the United States of America

ISBN 9781620043509

moon chilled

Caitlin Ricci

chapter one

Shae

My life isn't the conventional type of thing you'd expect from someone my age. The twenty-three-year-old women on TV are nothing like me. I've never been to a party, don't know the first thing about getting an education of any type, and my cell phone is a cheap prepaid thing that has barely enough money on it for one phone call. No, my life may not be the expectation of many, but for a werewolf, it's just fine.

I stepped out of the small hunting cabin I was renting and into a chilly winter morning in the Colorado Mountains. The cabin was barely big enough for the few pieces of furniture I had in it, none of which were mine. The human in me didn't mind the lack of space, and the wolf part of me had no use for material things. She could make do in most situations, and the small cabin was only of benefit to the human. My wolf would likely prefer it if we never stopped long enough to need a cabin in the first place. She was practical like that, often reminding me that clothes and other things humans seemed to hoard were of no importance to the likes of us. After all, we had our life, and anything else was just gravy.

As a human, I walked the mile into town with the night's frost clinging to my boots. They were worn, picked up in a back alley trashcan in one of the many towns I'd been visited during the last ten years of my life. They were a few sizes too big for me and likely belonged to a man at once point, but at least they weren't tight. And since I rarely wore them, or any other clothing for that matter, I figured I could put up with a bit of discomfort for the sake of looking like a human.

Whenever I was out in public, which admittedly wasn't very often, that was what I focused on. Humans, though similar to me, were fundamentally nothing like me. And I'd seen enough movies and read just as many books to know what humans did to something that wasn't like them. My wolf knew too, and it put her on the defensive as soon as we were within range of the town. She didn't like coming down here and protested loudly by bristling up and growling in the back of my mind. I pictured myself stroking my fingers through her fur, trying to calm her as she struggled for control over my body. This was a necessity, and though she couldn't understand why, she took my word for it. This time. I had no doubt that the next time I asked her to come down here wouldn't be so easy. We didn't need supplies; much of what I needed she and I could gather from the woods around us. Instead we had need of something that was purely human in design—money.

I detested the entire principle of it, likely by my wolf's influence, but the cabin we rented needed to be paid for with the flimsy paper bills, and so we did what we needed to in order to survive. As always. I had the distinct impression my wolf resented me for choosing to be human in this of all things. I tried not to let her opinion of the matter bother me. She was stubborn and could be arrogant at times. I liked to think I gave her that.

I walked into the grocery store and took a hard left at the first chance I could, putting me right by the bulletin board that hung beside the bathrooms. As I stood there and shifted my weight, my heavy winter coat was loud, swishing in the wind, I looked through the variety of livestock for sale ads and missing pet fliers to find the ones I wanted. I disliked wearing the coat, with its heavy zippers and other metal pieces that always seemed to make noise. But humans experienced the cold when there was snow on the ground, and I had to blend in. Still, I wasn't human, not even close, and so by the time I'd found a job that I could likely do, I was desperate to shed the jacket and as many other layers of clothing as I could manage.

As a wolf, I held none of the shame or uncertainty that humans seemed to experience when they went without clothing. I had very few pieces of clothing, as when I was alone I simply went without them. And because I was alone most of the time, there was little need for me to have the possessions that the humans I'd seen around me covet as if they were the most important thing in life.

I knew what was important to me, and she lived more than a day away in a town south of where I now stood. Even if she were closer, though, there were reasons we no longer spoke often, if at all. My past was not something that I chose to think about. But thinking of her made me remember it. There was no separating them. They simply existed together, no matter how much I tried to fight that fact.

Back to the matter at hand, I decided with a shake of my head as I tried to clear my mind. I tore the information for a job off one of the flyers. There were others posted, but only this one had nothing to do with animals, even though I knew they'd likely be in the vicinity. It wasn't that I didn't like the goats, horses, and cows that called the little mountain town home with me. But I was clearly a predator to them, and they seemed to realize this whenever I was close.

I'd considered taking a job housesitting for a person that had chickens once. My wolf barely resisted having one for lunch, but my letting them live hardly seemed to matter to the birds that had nearly hurt themselves in an effort to get away from me while I'd been collecting eggs for their owner.

My wolf didn't understand the need for money, and most of the time I agreed with her because I hardly thought about the stuff except when the rent came due. We ate what we caught, washed ourselves in the river, and slept outside for as many months as possible until the cold made such things impossible—which wasn't often, given how thick my wolf's fur is. My wolf would rather we live in a cave somewhere and never come near humans again. We'd tried that at first, when we were too young to rent a place and living with people had been out of the question. She'd loved the cave. I'd missed people. I suppose that's because, in the deepest parts of my heart, I know I'm not really a wolf and can never be one. Even if I let her have complete control, I'd only ever be a werewolf that was letting my wolf out to play.

But being completely human didn't work for us either, because I wasn't one of them. I thought of myself as special, even unique, in this little town. In the world of werewolves, I was only one in a large number of others. We aren't as rare as people may like to think. But here I was the only one. As far as I knew, anyway. I hadn't put up my own flyer asking to meet others like me. I wasn't that desperate to be called the crazy one and run out of town. Not when I'd made a decent life here for myself over the past few years.

I put the piece of the flyer with a farmer's name on it in my pocket. He was looking for someone to help him restore an old barn. Simple enough, I reasoned. I didn't know much about restoring old buildings, but I was stronger than most and rarely tired out for long. But I had no other options, and was rent coming due. My landlord liked getting his money, though why he insisted on it was beyond me. He gave me a discount for watching the place and keeping it tidy, but even though he'd said that he would be stopping by to use the hunting cabin on occasion, he never had.

A movie I'd watched the summer before suggested that sometimes women traded things for rent. I'd considered it, as trading was a form of commerce that both my wolf and I understood, until I was led to believe from the movie that this thing to trade was the woman's body. Both my wolf and I knew that was never going to happen. Some things were too awful to consider for long and were best left alone to rot in some deep, dark hole in the back of my mind. I preferred them that way.

With the man's number in my pocket, I left the store and instantly had to blink snow off my eyelashes as it came down on top of me. The storm had picked up, flakes coming down faster and dropping the temperature around me. My wolf saw snow and wanted to go play in it, to roll and run until we were cooled down and no longer sweating through this impossibly thick, noisy coat.

As much as I wanted to do just as she had suggested with her various images and gentle but persistent prodding into my thoughts, we had other things to do at the moment. Getting this job happened to be one of them.

Without any form of identification or proof that I'd ever attended school, which I hadn't, getting something that people might consider a real job was impossible. Documents could be forged; the little amount of TV that I was able to get through the antenna attached to the cabin had told me so. But the shows I watched made it seem like that task required money, which I didn't have, and expertise, of which I was sorely lacking. And so I took the jobs I could around town when the rent came due. Work was better in the spring when people had planting to do, or in the fall when someone would be out hunting and needed a bit of help. I wasn't a guide—nothing near that official. But I knew where the deer liked to graze and the trails the elk took.

The barn owner would likely be looking for men to come and offer him their help. Fighting for respect wasn't anything new for me. I knew I looked younger than I was, and as a girl, the men in town underestimated me. It had been that way no matter where I went, and it didn't bother me. Usually, anyway. Sometimes being treated as a stupid little girl without a brain or any sort of thoughts of my own got old. But after being on my own for so long I was nearly used to it. At least it wasn't as bad as it had been.

I would tone it down for the farmer. By 'it,' I meant everything about me. My strength, my speed, my intelligence. I was naturally better than the humans that lived near me because I was a predator. But he didn't need to know that. I'd show him that I wasn't some weak little girl, but I wouldn't give myself away either. It was a delicate process, one that I wasn't all that good at. I'd try my best, though. I had to. Before moving to this forgotten little mountain town, I'd lived a bit further east in a place called Loveland. It had been smaller than Denver, but there were still more people than I was used to being around. This was back when I was still trying to pretend to be completely normal, when I thought that maybe someday I might even get my GED and go to college and have a real job where I had to wear shoes and such, possibly even a badge. Once, years ago, I'd thought that fighting the bad guys would be a fun way to make a living. Like on the cop shows I'd caught on occasion. But I knew myself well enough to figure out I didn't play well with others or within the rules. There were certain people in this world that I wouldn't be able to stop my wolf from attacking and I wouldn't have wanted her to, either.

Anyway, I'd been renting a room in this guy's townhouse, which should have sent off warning bells, but I figured I could handle it. I'd done more than my fair share of handling things by that time. I didn't expect him to consider sex a fair trade for rent, though I guess I should have known something was off, since the interview he had with me had consisted of a bunch of what I realized later on were pretty personal questions. What did I sleep in, was I dating anyone, that sort of thing. Weird, right? Very. But whatever; I was only eighteen, and though I had plenty of experience in the world, not much of it was with other people.

Long story short, I guess I should mention that he spent a week in the hospital, and I broke my lease by being gone before he got out. The cop shows I watch sometimes made it seem like he might have pressed charges or maybe I had a warrant out or something, but I hadn't been in a big town since then, so I really wasn't sure. If the cops were after me, I knew nothing about it, and so I pretended that they weren't. Besides, if they were, I could shift and simply run away from them. Because of my wolf's influence, I had always been much better at hiding in the woods than any humans I have ever met.

Though there'd been a few months, back when I was thirteen and already feeling far older than my years, that I hadn't trusted myself or my wolf. We were alone, living in the summertime woods on the western slope of the Colorado Mountains, living off berries and the few fish that I'd been able to catch. Too weak to fight her off, my wolf came out. I remember crying after that first shift. I was sore and stiff, and walking on paws was a completely new experience for me. But she kept me alive through the fall, and by the time that winter hit I was more than ready to let her come out to play. I was fourteen then and more of an adult than any of the older teenagers I briefly encountered in my one trip to the mall—

which was some sort of hell on earth, as far as I was concerned. It was noisy and crowded, not to mention completely enclosed with no real room to run or hide if I needed to get away. That wasn't an experience I'd be going through again if I could help it.

I'd felt old since I had first stepped foot outside of the pack I'd belonged to at the time. I was glad to leave them, but I'd grown up fast as a child out on my own. If I hadn't had my wolf inside me, giving me strength and telling me that I couldn't give up because I didn't have a choice and she wasn't going to die with me, I don't know if I could have made it through. I like to tell myself that I could have been just fine. But I know the truth. I needed her, and still do. I wouldn't have lived through my first fall without her there to help me.

Keeping my head down, I walked quickly past a car parked in front of the old hardware store. It was idling and a woman was sitting in the front seat and I could see her watching me curiously, like most of the people in this little town did. I was fine being the weirdo girl that lived in the hunting cabin outside of town. It kept me safe. Attention wasn't something that I needed, but money often was. Once a month, anyhow. I hunted for what I could, stole when I had to—which was rarely, since if I got caught it meant more attention on me—and dealt with any lack between the two however I had to. There was nothing particularly glamorous about my life. I bathed in cool rivers, ate dinner on my paws with my face buried in a fresh kill, and slept in an old mattress with so many smells in it that I had to use cotton balls stuffed up my nose to be able to sleep through the night. Which was why I rarely slept in the cabin unless it was too cold for me to do otherwise. It was rare, but I preferred to sleep in there with the old wood stove to keep me warm rather than shiver under the snow as my wolf.

I didn't need much in life, likely because I'd gone so long without. Ten long years of being on my own had given me quite a bit of perspective when it came to material things. I did need one thing in this world, but the tawny wolf whose image instantly came to my mind couldn't be helped. She was too far away and long ago lost to me, despite what our bond said. I tried not to think about her too often, but when two people were as connected as us, it was hard not to. I missed her every minute of every day and had done so since the terrible night when I'd had to leave her behind. I shook my head and tried not to think about those thoughts. They wouldn't do me any good, after all.

My mate couldn't be saved. Not while she chose to live with that pack, to be with him. I missed her and wished that I could have her by my side. Wished that we could play in the summer sun and run around laughing and chasing each other like we had when we were children. She was my mate, my own true love, and the compliment to my withered soul. If I had such a thing. But she couldn't be saved.

No, that was a lie. And one I'd been fighting with myself for years about. Maiki could be freed; she could be mine again. If I were willing to go back there. But that would never happen again. I could not live in that pack. I would not. I'd run from there for a reason, and I would never be going back. I swore that to myself, and though it meant keeping us apart, I'd had to be selfish just that once in order to keep myself safe. Even though it hurt more than I could possibly bear.

I let the chill of the mountain air fill my lungs as I thought. Of course the ridiculous idea that it wouldn't be that hard to go back came into my mind. I let the idea fall away. Going back wasn't an option if I wanted to stay alive. I knew this and knew what was waiting for me back there if I ever did return. I had seen him enough in my nightmares over the years that I didn't need to see him with my eyes as well. Maiki was lost to me. Forever. The sooner I let that idea settle inside myself and give up hope, the better off I'd be.

And yet I'd sent a letter with my new phone number to her just the summer before. It was probably stupid, but the human part of me couldn't let it go. Or maybe it was that my wolf refused to believe that Maiki was lost to us. Either way, I'd put in the effort and made sure to have my phone on me when I wasn't letting my wolf out just in case she called. She hadn't contacted me since the night I'd left. I didn't even know if she still even lived there. She was alive; I was sure of that much, at least. But more than that, I couldn't tell. It was enough for me, most of the time, just to know that she was alive. I didn't know if she was safe, but alive was close enough, I guessed. For me it had to be.

I wrestled with the idea of going back to my little hunting cabin. I had an old book or two there that I could read again and enough logs to make a quick fire. I even had a few bags of tea remaining from the time I'd indulged and purchased the box because it was on sale and the grocery store manager was watching me too closely for me to steal it. An evening in was starting to sound nice. But my wolf wanted none of it. She didn't even want to consider the idea, even when I offered to let her take over so that she could lie inside the heated cabin as well. But she wanted to run, to explore, to see what she could with her predator's gaze. There were elk nearby, and she wanted to see if their numbers were larger than the small group that had moved through the week before. I knew that she intended to hunt if there was a young one there that would make an easy meal. She didn't hunt big game often; to do so would be wasteful when we were the only large predator in the area to enjoy the kill.

My wolf did not waste food, no matter how easy the catch. It had taken me a while to understand that after she'd refused to take over my body and come out to take on an injured bull elk. He would have been a quick, easy kill. But his meat would have gone to waste as well, and his death would have meant little. Respect in all things, she'd taught me. A life was a precious thing, and taking one just because I could was not allowed. We'd gone hungry that night, but I had learned my lesson well enough and hadn't questioned her judgment after that. She spotted the food, I let her take over if she wasn't doing so already, and then we ate.

The parts we couldn't eat like the bones and skins we sold to the taxidermist in the next town over so that he could stuff them and mount them as some sort of macabre trophies onto the wall. He didn't question us on where we got our animals and never once bothered to see my hunting permit. I guess that's because he realized I didn't have one. He probably thought I was odd, especially since I had known nothing about guns when he'd wondered what I had used to bring the first elk down. I didn't know what he paid everyone else, but I guessed that it was more than what I got for my skins and antlers. I didn't let it bother me, since it wasn't as if I needed the money for something aside from rent. My utilities were covered by my rent, and my only outside cost, my phone, had the same amount of minutes on it since the day I'd purchased it.

My simple little life wouldn't have worked for most people. But they weren't a werewolf hiding out in plain sight amongst a bunch of mountain humans either.

My wolf persisted, telling me again that she wanted to hunt today. I worked to calm her the best I could. It worked, just barely. But I knew she'd still want to do something. She got bored easily when she didn't have a task. And it had been a good week since I'd let her out to hunt. In the winter, when food was far scarcer than any other time of the year, I didn't let her out as often. It took too much energy, and without something to hunt on the largely deserted mountain, there wasn't any point. I'd gone a week without food before, though it had hurt and I wouldn't recommend it. But when I had to, I knew that I could.

"I'll let you out soon," I whispered, giving her that promise. But it would not be today, and it absolutely wouldn't be so close to town. We'd tracked a small buck to the outside of a rancher's farm over the summer. As a wolf, I look like any other out there in the world, and so the rancher had tried to shoot at me. I was fast and he was a bad shot, but it was far too close of a call for me to forget it anytime soon.

He'd only seen a wolf near his cattle; I couldn't very well blame him. He didn't know that my tastes went to the far gamier than a simple side of beef, but she'd made sure to stay well away from the rancher's property after that. It was far too dangerous—I couldn't very well go to a hospital and somehow explain a gunshot wound.

The more I thought about it, the more I didn't want to spend the day cooped up in the cabin. It was a decent enough space, for a human, and I did still want a quiet evening with a cup of tea, a warm fire, and a good book. But I could get those things later. With it being winter I spent far too much time in the cabin anyway. My wolf and I liked the sun on our backs, the rush of racing through the fallen leaves, and feeling the mountain air on our skin. No, we wouldn't be going back to the cabin so soon. Not when there was a whole world to explore.

I calmed my wolf the best I could, reminding her that although there were places that we hadn't yet explored in town, we wouldn't be going near them either. It was too dangerous. My wolf understood self-preservation, likely more than I did, but she was still a risk-taker in places where I wasn't. She was faster than I was and could blend in easily with the white forest around us. But I didn't want to risk the people in town putting out traps for us. Getting caught was definitely not to my list of things to do that day, not that I often had a list. Going out and deciding what I wanted to do from each moment to the next was far more my speed. There was less stress that way, or at least I thought so. I watched the people go back and forth to their jobs, to the grocery store, to get gas in their cars. And I wondered how they did it. And why they put up with it. I liked my way a lot more.

With excess energy still thick in my veins, I took off into the higher places in the winter forest. I went off the trails, stayed away from the homes high on cliffs surrounded by woods, and began to run. I raced over fallen trees and around bright white Aspens, shivering in the cold wind. My boots were heavy, and I wished for the feeling of the snow and ice against my toes but knew better than to risk it as I took a sharp corner and leapt over a rock shaped like a giant frog. I misjudged the ground on the other side of the frog and ended up sliding down the hill. I rolled, fallen leaves sticking in my hair as I tried my best to avoid hitting any downed trees. At the end of the steep hill I rolled haphazardly onto my back and, with my face red and my hair a mess, I gave a mighty whooping cry of joy.

I sat up and spent a good chunk of time, until the sun had fallen in the sky, getting the leaves out of the tangled mess my hair had become. I used to care more about my appearance. Back when Maiki had told me I was beautiful; when she had sat behind me, quietly brushing out my hair and humming to me a lullaby she said came from her mother but I suspected was just something she'd made up. I met her mother only once a couple of weeks before her death. My own father died shortly after that. Maiki's mother hadn't seemed like the kind of woman to sing at all, much less a lullaby to her only child.

"Big moon in the sky, guide this child, love her, keep her, raise her, something ... something, something," I whispered to the falling snow. I didn't know the rest of the words to Maiki's lullaby and wasn't even sure if those that I thought I did remember were correct.

My hair was longer, and darker, than the last time Maiki had seen it. That simple thought brought a wave of memories and remembered sensations that I braced myself against. I'd held her hand, kissed her cheek, lied next to her in the summer sun. We'd been thirteen and perfectly, blissfully happy for one brief shining moment in our young lives.

Before everything had changed so dramatically. I got up and pressed my hand against the stiff, biting bark of a nearby tree. A buck had rubbed part of it down, exposing the soft underside of the bark but also leaving the rest of it rough. I didn't mind the pain as I pushed my hand against that bark. In fact, I welcomed it for the escape it brought. In that moment of pain I was able to forget, to focus on the pain in my hand and not the remembered pain of a night long ago. It was simply me, alone in a forest full of snow and trees far older than I was. And I took some comfort in that solitude.

My energy spent, I pulled away from the tree and started walking back down the hill. I'd gone up far, much more so than I'd meant to, and the climb down required my focus to not slip and fall. I appreciated that I needed to concentrate and gave it my all, focusing on my task even in the smallest detail, until Maiki in the form of her tawny wolf took her place at the back of my mind, once again giving me peace in a world full of noise and pain. The last time I'd seen her hadn't been so blissful, though. I remembered everything in perfect, horrific clarity, but most of all I remembered running. I'd gone as far east as possible, but somehow I'd always known that my home was in the Colorado Rockies, so I'd never really been able to get all that far away. Anything without mountains felt too flat. I'd made it as far as the Kansas border before turning around and racing back. There'd been no trees, no elk, no crystal-clear and bone-chillingly cold streams full of mountain trout. The entire place had felt far too alien to me; I'd refused to leave again, knowing right where my home, my territory, was.

Once I'd reached the edge of the forest I had a choice to make. Back to the cabin, where I was sure my memories would come to torment me once again, or to find the man's barn that needed some repairs and see if he'd let me do a bit of work today. I chose the easy answer and started heading back toward town, as much as I disliked being around all the humans and their busy little lives.

My wolf gave me the sense that I had been foolish to waste my energy reserves on my run. I even agreed with her. My wolf was right, or she would have been in that we'd only had fresh kills to rely on for our food. But there was a grocery store, and I had a little money for canned foods. Or I could always steal them, if I got desperate enough. Revolting as my wolf thought that idea was, I knew that we'd survived on food out of cans before. It hadn't been for very long, and I'd felt weak after more than a month of it. But, though hunting came naturally to my kind, I hadn't been allowed to practice those skills as a child and even the basics had been a learning experience for me. Like everything else in my life after leaving the pack, hunting had come quickly to me. As had stealing when money was as scarce as prey. Survival was my only option, and I knew that I could, and would, do whatever was necessary to achieve it.

chapter two

Shae

It took me a good half hour to find the man's barn, likely because everything looked the same with so much snow on it, but eventually I did manage to find a building that looked similar to the picture of the barn posted on the flyer. Only that picture was obviously taken years before, as the barn I currently stood beside was in serious need of some new boards and a few dozen nails. I approached from the south as the wind was blowing at my back. I was not hunting, and the horses in the corral attached to the barn needed to know that as I came toward them. Like many little girls, I'd loved horses growing up. Even now that I knew I could never come within five feet of one of the beautiful animals, I still found their beauty to be nearly overwhelming and envied the people that were able to ride them as this man and his family must.

The scent of hay and leather was almost comforting as I stood watching the nearest horse. My wolf was cautious, as suspicious as she was of all humans. I didn't share her concerns and wished my wolf spirit inside of me would find a nice place in the back of my mind to fall asleep for a little while. True, humans could be dangerous, and we'd met our fair share of them over the years at bus stations and in back alleys in the few times we'd ventured into the city. But that was when I'd been a child, lost and alone in a world I'd never experienced before. I'd been frightened then, afraid of everything, including my own shadow. And my wolf had been my comforter, my protector, my sense of strength in the quiet of the night when I'd had nothing to protect me from the wind and the only meal I could find were the rats that ran across my bare feet.

However, now that I was grown, I knew that there was only one true monster in this world, and he was nowhere near here. I'd made sure of that. Moving closer to the little house, away from the shelter of the forest that I could have easily backed into and blended in with, I tried to look and act like a human. Sure, I looked the part well enough. But there were differences, however subtle they were. They were still there, and I had to be cautious and mindful of them at all times. The people of this little town likely thought a young woman living all alone in a hunting cabin deep in the woods was strange to begin with. I didn't need them coming after me with pitchforks and torches.

I ignored the horses that lifted their heads and snorted at me. I was a predator, regardless of my human clothing, and they were prey, even though she'd never hunted one of them and in truth had no interest in doing so. I'd fallen in love with horses from the first time I'd been allowed to watch movies with my favorite horse heroes in them. They raced across deserts and carried men into battle, and in the quiet of the night when the TV had been turned off I went to my boxes of books, all with the same horse theme, and dove into their worlds. That had been before coming to the pack, back when my parents had both been alive, back when I'd been simply a werewolf child with a family to call my own and my biggest problem had been not getting the cereal I wanted for breakfast. I'd spent many nights reading about horses and wishing I could ride them. But unlike most children, I'd never grown out of my obsession. That I'd never been less than five feet from one didn't really matter to me; I still adored them and wished that I could ride one, just once.

"Easy," I said to one of the closest horses. He was a fuzzy, stout gelding with a heavy winter blanket on. I knew that was what people said to frightened horses, and had I been human, maybe it would have worked. But I wasn't, and the horse's wide, frightened eyes only grew bigger until it looked like there was no more room left for his pupils. He turned to face me with steam came out from his quivering nostrils. He looked cold and I pitied him, even with his heavy winter coat and blanket on.

I heard footsteps and the slamming of a door before I ever saw a man come out of the house to my right. He walked toward me, his boots sounding heavy as they crunched through the snow. His strides were long, and his face, what I could see of it under the thick ski mask he wore, looked twisted in anger. But there was concern in his old eyes. Whether it was for himself, his horses, or the woman and young children I could hear inside, I didn't know.

"You there!" he called, once he was close enough that he probably thought I could hear him. I had first heard him inside, though, just as I could also hear the TV playing and the laughter of his children as they sat around it singing along to the show's theme song. "What are you doing near my horses?"

He had a shotgun in his hand. It hung loosely at his side; easy to use from that position. Though even if he had it up and pointed directly at me I doubt he could have killed me with it. I'm a bit faster than a normal human's aim when I really want to be. I knew that humans were fast with their guns, especially up here where they had to use them to defend their homes and livestock from predators much more dangerous than I am. But I was fast too, and I was fairly confident of my ability to get to cover and hide before he could kill me. If he got lucky, though, a gunshot would hurt. It wouldn't likely kill me, but I was in no way immortal, and I did not feel like taking the time to stitch myself up again. The last time hadn't gone so well for me, and the puffy, red scar hurt sometimes.

I had to say something, anything more than *please don't shoot me*, but nothing came to mind. I stood there in the snow staring at him and attempting to judge his next movements so that I could act accordingly. "I was saying hello; this one was frightened. I didn't want him to spook and hurt himself if he slipped on the ice," I answered him honestly after a long stretch of silence.

I imagined what the man could see with his human eyes when he looked at me and wondered which version of myself I wanted to show him. I gave him what I considered my human look, battling back my wolf in me until she was contented to simply look through my eyes rather than be evident in them. I was a young woman of barely twenty with long, dark brown hair, and though I had muscles to spare, they were hidden under a jacket. I wasn't tall or big, and I'd been told that I looked even younger than I was.

In short, I wasn't all that impressive but hoped he'd see past that if I decided to offer my help to him. I hadn't yet decided on that matter. I understood the man's thought process in going for his gun, since I was a stranger to most of the people in this little town, but I hoped he didn't think that I was a threat to him. I preferred to be a stranger to them all; fewer connections meant that I could leave instantly if I needed to with only my landlord to miss me. And I wasn't entirely sure how I felt about a possible employer holding a gun on me, even if he wasn't pointing it directly at me.

He shook his head, seeming to come back to himself. The gun shook in his hand, and I considered bolting but decided against it. For the moment at least I'd stay. "You can't be here. Go on, get."

The corners of my mouth pulled down into a frown as I stood there considering him and his demands. An icy wind blew around me as it swept through the valley. "I came for the job." I fished the torn piece of paper with his number on it from her pocket and held it out for him to see. I didn't move toward him, though, as I saw his hand tighten on the butt of the gun.

He didn't come closer, but he did stare at me and the piece of paper in my outstretched hand. After a moment or two, his gaze softened, and he relaxed the hand around his gun to the point where I almost thought it might slip through his fingers. "It's freezing out here. And aren't you a bit young for work like this? It's hard labor and I won't pay much. Not my fault if you get hurt out here." His voice had gone from angry, to mildly curious, to completely distrustful.

I smiled, though not too much. Big smiles were scary to humans and a challenge to people like me. I'd learned that early on. My kind liked their tight little smiles and subtle signs of affection. I couldn't remember a time when I'd ever seen two werewolves run to each other and do the strange flying hug thing I saw in the movies I watched. Research for fitting in, I called them. So I gave him a tiny smile and shifted my weight. My wolf could hold still for hours. Humans weren't like that. I had to remember to move, to fidget. It made me look more like them, and that was the whole point to this, wasn't it? His concern was more for himself than for me, and I knew that. But I still smiled anyway because I thought it was what was expected of me.

"If you give me a chance I'll make it worth your while," I offered in flat, even tones. I wasn't afraid of work, of getting dirty, or of the possibility of becoming hurt while doing this job. My wolf came forward and protested that idea. She wasn't afraid of a little pain either, but she wouldn't go seeking it, and right then she was adamant about simply disappearing into the woods and forgetting all about the cabin and rent altogether. Her way would be much simpler. But I was a werewolf, a child born of two worlds, and I had to figure out the line for myself sometimes.

He hesitated, though he did seem to consider it for a moment but then started to shake his head. Before he could, I stopped him with an offer I hoped he couldn't refuse. I hated to do it, especially because I knew I deserved, and was worth, more. But there weren't all that many options, especially in the winter months, and though I hadn't been sure of offering to work for him, I knew that rent had to be paid, so I made up my mind. I could be picky during the spring, fall, and summer. This time of year, things were tight for everyone and money was scarce. I hoped he didn't see how desperate I was. "I'll take two dollars less per hour than your offered pay."

That seemed to change his mind in a hurry; his brows lifted into his tattered ball cap and he rocked back on his heels a bit. He looked toward the house behind him. I looked too and saw the outline of a woman through the drawn, checkered yellow curtains. "Because you're a girl?" he asked me, as if that wasn't already the obvious reason for my lower offer.

I pushed the instant thought of Maiki to the back of my mind. If she'd been here I would have had a different thought process, a different reason for doing this. But she wasn't; there was just me here as I tried to make this broken life work for myself.

More like I was desperate, but I wasn't about to let him know that. Letting him believe what he wanted to, I simply nodded. My work, if he let me show it to him, I knew would prove my worth. And I preferred actions to words so much more anyway, regardless of the situation. Actions just made sense in a way that words simply never had to me. Besides, looking desperate only brought pity. Or, in my experience, it brought out the predator in people that would only try to take advantage of me. Neither option really appealed to me on such a frosty afternoon.

"What's your name?" he asked me, his voice still hard and distrusting. One of the horses snorted and pawed at the ground as if irritated, but if it was by the cold, the snow getting into his eyes, or by my presence, I didn't really know.

"Shae Lobo," I replied, the name falling easily off my lips after so many years of using it. The first name was correct, but the last was a whole different matter.

He cocked his head to the side, and the gun slipped a few inches in his hand until the point, the end I wanted to stay as far away from as possible, wasn't trained on me. "Like a wolf?"

I shrugged and made sure to keep his gaze. Looking away was akin to lying to some of these humans. "Just my name." Not many people connected my chosen last name with what it meant, though the translation wasn't exactly rare. I tried not to look surprised that he'd figured it out. After all, it meant nothing. It was just a name like any other. And I knew that I'd never hunted on his property. I was careful about where I went when I was a wolf, and horses, like dogs, were too good of a warning system for me to walk close to them without being discovered.

After a long moment in which he stared at me and I tried not to let the attention get to me, he nodded and took a step back, appearing to be satisfied with our exchange. "You'll find wood stacked in the barn along with a hammer and a coffee can of nails. The outside of the barn is nearly done, but the inside needs to be completely redone. It's been stripped, though, so just line the boards up like they already are in the empty stalls and hammer them in.

The horses come in at sunset so you'll have to stop then. You sure you know what you're doing here? If you screw it up, you won't be paid." His voice had gone hard again, and I bristled, my head lowering.

My wolf didn't like the insult to us either, and if she'd been out, her ears would have been back. I could picture her like that, from the few times I'd seen her reflection in the clear waters of the stream that ran past the cabin in the summer. She was a deep charcoal gray, the kind of color found only after everything else in the fire had burned down and only ash and crumbled bits of dying embers were left. Our eyes were the same, though, the same odd shade of a deep, rich amber that was not normally found in humans but fairly common in wolves.

I smirked and worked to calm my wolf before she could get upset within my mind. She was not to teach this man a lesson about underestimating us. We weren't insulted by his questions; we forgave him for his ignorance and would move on. My wolf, stubborn beast that she was, took a bit longer to convince than I did. I simply understood that showing this man what I could do would be a better threat to his narrow little worldview than shifting and biting him would be. "I do," I told him. He didn't look convinced, but after a long moment in which he continued to stare at me, he turned around and gave me his back. It wasn't a smart thing to do to a predator, but I didn't have the urge to chase him and hunt him down. If he'd been a weak, injured deer that was running from me, I wouldn't have resisted. That would have been a good, merciful kill, and I would have made it neat and clean.

The back door closed and I shook my head, getting my mind out of the hunting space it had drifted into. I was not hunting. I was working with my hands, like a human. The reminder helped get my wolf under control as well. The thought of hunting had reminded her that there were horses nearby. They were trapped and fat from a heavy winter feeding. They'd make an easy meal, my wolf was trying to say as she sent me the suggestion to hunt them, even though it was a lazy thought that I doubted she really meant. Prey was still prey and the easier it was to bring down, the more my wolf was interested. Especially when she knew that these horses didn't belong on her mountain. There were wild horses somewhere in Colorado but they weren't here and these horses weren't Mustangs. My wolf wanted them gone. I didn't bother trying to convince her otherwise. I simply ignored her. She knew my stance on eating horses when there was canned food available back at the cabin.

With him back in his house and surrounded by his family, I made my way into the barn. There was a metal gate that I had to go through since the barn didn't have an actual door. Before I got started, I took off my jacket. The lack of doors on either end of the barn created a tunnel for the wind to whip through and blast against me and the few horses that were brave enough to risk coming closer in order to find shelter under the edge of the roof off the barn. I breathed a sigh of relief as I took the jacket off and left it hanging on top of a saddle resting on a long wooden peg just inside the entrance of the barn.

I ignored the wind as it picked up outside, howling through the pine trees and young Aspens as I picked up the closest long board, lifted it easily, and began hammering it into the open space on the wall. It wasn't hard work at all, and I wondered why the man needed help as I moved onto the next board in the pile at my feet. Maybe the slight hitch my wolf had noticed in his step as he'd walked away had something to do with it. Either way, it wasn't my businesses why he needed someone to do this for him. I was simply grateful to be given the chance, and I was there strictly to work and get some money for rent. Stealing would have been preferred, but I couldn't exactly steal the cabin for the next month, and to do so would be far too risky. And in the quiet of this work, my wolf relaxed her restless pacing and settled into the back of my mind, seeming content with my usefulness—for a while, at least.

chapter three

Maiki

I woke up with sweat beaded on my forehead and the last tendrils of a nightmare snaking through my brain. I rolled over, wishing I was still asleep but knowing that if I closed my eyes again, the dream would be there waiting for me. Only it wasn't a dream. I'm a seer, and I know the difference between the nightmares of my past and the ones that have yet to come true. When I was a child, I'd wished to be able to see my own death, just so that I could know what age I would be when it happened. Then I could have looked forward to that year, counted down to it and celebrated its coming as a way to escape this madness. But my dreams didn't work like that, and I had someone else to live for now, to take care of. Someone that needed me just as much as I did him.

Deciding to get up, I pulled the thin crocheted blanket off me and rose to my feet at the side of the little twin bed I'd had since I was five. It hadn't been new then, and the years since hadn't been kind to it. But it served its purpose as well as anything else, I suppose. A picture caught my eye as I brushed my short blonde hair away from my face. Two little girls smiled back at me, both looking happy in that one perfect moment. Shae and another girl that looked like a younger, better version of me. But I hadn't been that other girl in over ten years.

I went out of my room and into the tiny bathroom across the hall to get ready. There wasn't much hot water left for a shower, but by now I was used to that. I got up later than everyone else, no matter how much I tried not to. I just wasn't a morning person, I guess.

A quick shower, a minute or two to brush my teeth, and I was back in my room to put something on. I had no idea what, though, and my lack of choices had nothing to do with the laundry not being done. I did it daily. No, my mediocre closest was a result of not being given a new outfit in more than three years. I pulled down a yellow dress and quickly slipped it on over my head. No one would care that I didn't have a bra on. It's not like I really have breasts anyway. The dress had been patched in a few places, but it fell past my knees and was one of the more modest things I owned.

I could smell the snow outside, the fresh blanket calling me to come out and play, but if I did, the dress wouldn't be any good for staying warm. But I was to stay inside most of the time and knew I wouldn't be let out unless the situation called for it. Which it rarely did. I brushed my hair quickly and hoped I looked like I'd gotten more sleep than I actually had. After that I left my room and walking down a few doors in the farmhouse's upstairs hallway with its peeling paint and creaking floors. It was larger than most like it, I supposed, since it had nearly five bedrooms, all of which were filled by my alpha and his favorite men. That I'd been good enough to deserve my own room had been a surprise. I figured that I owed that special treatment to the little boy who lay sleeping behind the door I knocked on.

I could hear his snores and let myself in, eager to see him and get him ready for the day. People were downstairs and knew I'd be needed soon. *Just a few more minutes*, I silently asked whoever might be listening. A little more time to start my day, to pretend things were good, that we were a normal little family. Instead of whatever it was that we'd become.

Gavin was stretched out on his own little twin bed. He'd been graduated to it only the month before, and compared to the toddler bed he'd been sleeping in this one looked as if it nearly swallowed him whole. I knelt on the bed beside him, his face only inches from mine. He was my perfect little boy, the son I hadn't expected to ever want. I didn't let that stray thought stay in my head long, as I knew of the kind of heartbreak it could bring to me if I let it fester. Instead I kissed his cheek, waking him up, and brushed his pale blond hair away from his head.

"Hey, sleepy," I said to him as soon as his eyes were open.

"Not yet, Mommy," he grumbled, trying to turn away from me. I wished that I could let him sleep, that he could have a few minutes simply just to enjoy himself. But that wasn't to be. We had things to do, he and I, and staying in bed wasn't one of them. And so I scooped him up, despite his protests, and set him down on his feet on the floor in front of me.

"C'mon." I took his hand and took him into the bathroom. His routine was easy, but getting him to brush his teeth wasn't a chore either of us enjoyed. Still, we managed to get it done without having the toothpaste squirt over either one of us in the struggle, and so I counted that as a win.

I took him downstairs and did my best to avoid being stepped on or run over by the much bigger men that were already filling the small kitchen. There wasn't a chair left for Gavin, so I lifted him onto the countertop, the design of which reminded me of the fifties, but not in a good way. It had none of the retro charm I saw in the magazines I snuck sometimes from other members of the pack. It just looked old and really worn down. I pulled a juice box out of the fridge for Gavin before getting started on the breakfast orders for the people I was responsible for feeding.

It wasn't everyone, I wasn't running a cafeteria, after all, but there were plenty of people to feed anyway. Soon I had a handful of skillets out, each on a burner as I scrambled eggs and cooked up bacon. I never really noticed it as a child, but now that I was cooking for them, I had to say that werewolves ate far more than their bodies should have been able to. I didn't know where all that food went; I just went with it, pulling out another dozen eggs when the first were gone. I just cooked for them, didn't ask questions, and was glad someone had remembered to go get the eggs from the chickens in the side yard this morning. That was not one of my jobs, even though it could have been and was in the past. Taking care of Gavin had replaced many of my responsibilities in the pack. I guess I was lucky to have given birth to a son.

The first row of plates was placed on the table, and I waited for the next batch of food to cook. Gavin was done with his juice box so I gave him a bag of peeled oranges I'd tried to get him to eat yesterday.

He would have rather had the cookies I made last night, but that wasn't going to happen until after lunch at the earliest. He had a sweet tooth as bad as mine.

I heard voices coming through the back door as men entered the house. I didn't need to look up at them to know who they were. My nose told me all of that. I dropped my gaze and stepped back, allowing my alpha and his closest men through. They came into the kitchen, and I backed into the nearest corner, staying out of their way but close enough if needed. My alpha was with them, and I ducked my head, averting my eyes for him most of all.

They smelled of the wind and mountain snow, and something else, something I dared not put a name to so early in the day. I avoided them and tried not to let their casual brushes against what little exposed skin I had bother me. They were in charge and could do as they wished, with or without my consent.

"Hello, boy," my alpha said, going to my son and patting him on his shoulder. He wasn't affectionate with him, not as I thought a father should be. But then again, he'd never actually wanted a child, and if Gavin had been born female, I didn't know ... That was not a thought for today, and I quickly put it away in favor of something lighter, something much more fitting for this chilly morning. The sun was out, and its glare against the bright white snow made me blink before I turned away from the window where the curtains had been pulled back to allow in the light. The mountain was beautiful, the snow a welcome reminder of the season. And I had my son. That there was a space missing in my heart didn't matter.

Nothing could fill that hole, but thinking about it did no one any good, especially when her name wasn't to be mentioned in this pack.

"Sir?" I spoke up, knowing that I needed to tell my alpha about my dreams as soon as I saw him in the mornings, no matter what else he was doing. That was his rule. And I might not get another chance to do so. He often went hunting in the afternoons or was otherwise engaged. I didn't look up, but I didn't have to in order to know he was against the back wall. Years of living with them had given me decent spatial recognition as a matter of survival. I had to get his attention, but he wasn't looking at me. He was talking with one of his men in front of the fridge. I knew him, knew his smell and too much else about him as well. I did not go toward him. But I needed my alpha to notice me. I touched his elbow, the barest touch possible, before pulling back.

"Yes?" he demanded, his voice stern, bringing the noise in the kitchen to a halt around us. No one moved when he spoke. But it wasn't out of respect. The people in my pack feared him, and I knew first-hand that it was with good reason. While women and children were far more often the focus of his attention, men hardly went without a scratch in our little pack.

With his attention turned to me, I went to my knees in the kitchen. Not because he'd demanded it or because he'd even said anything to me that would suggest it. Not yet, anyway. But because the strength of my alpha's attention on me made it impossible for me to do anything else.

I pulled my shoulders down and in and hugged my arms against my stomach. Talking to him always made me feel a bit queasy. "I had a dream last night," I said, trying to get my voice to be louder, but it didn't work.

He made an irritated noise in his throat. "A what?"

I curled my hands against the edge of the counter, needing its strength to keep my balance, even on my knees. "A dream." My free hand went to my knee, and my fingers disappeared under the hem of the dress I wore. "I had a dream last night." I whispered the words, half-afraid to voice them. More than half, if I were being honest with myself. Which, I realized with no small amount of disgust, I hadn't been all that much lately. Some things were simply too hard to do and I, the weakest member of our pack, knew that better than most.

"Tell me about this dream you had, seer," he said, his voice soft, coaxing me into a deceptive calm. I knew better than to believe him, but I knew even more that fighting him would end up being worse for me. And though I wasn't sure how much Gavin knew, I was sure he'd never seen what our alpha was capable of. Not first-hand, at the very least. I was sure of that.

I didn't want to tell him, and I lowered my head even further toward the cracked and peeling linoleum floor to get away from the whispered command in his seemingly innocent words. I knew not telling him would make him mad, but the dream would upset him more. I didn't know what to do. Shae would have, had she been here, but I wasn't Shae and I didn't have the answers. My hair, short and blonde, fell into my eyes to brush against the floor. I was momentarily distracted by how brittle it was, how frail the dull yellow strands were, before I felt the floor below my fingertips vibrate as he stepped forward, his heavy boots carrying him toward me. I held still, knowing that if I shrank away when he was this close and could see me doing so that it would mean trouble for me. And my back had only just finished healing from my last punishment when I'd washed a dry clean-only dress belonging to one of the girls in the pack.

But I also didn't just want to sit there, to welcome his touch even while I secretly reviled it. But inaction was the same as allowing it. Or so I'd always thought. I didn't want him that close to me, and the thought of being touched by him made me want to spill what little breakfast I'd been able to manage up until then onto the floor. It was hard enough being in the same room, the same house, as him, and having him this close was nearly unbearable.

His smell, his touch; they brought back memories that I didn't want to remember. Things I'd been trying to block away since I was a child. But they were too many to count, and his proximity made them come close to the surface, back to where they could be seen again, to be relived in a way I never wanted to again. I'd barely survived them once—I couldn't do it again. I didn't have the strength to weather them a second time around. There was a distant rumble in the back of my mind, something wanting to be remembered but too long ignored and forgotten to bring back so easily. My nightmare memories took energy and time I didn't have to spare, and so I fought them even as I saw him reach toward me, his old, withered fingertips like claws coming at me.

His rough, calloused fingers landed on the back of my neck, just below the line of my short hair, and my breath caught in that moment between life and what could certainly be a quick death, if that was what my alpha wanted from me. His fingers tightened on the fine hairs at my nape, and I closed my eyes, squinting against the fear, the pain, and everything I imagined death to be. I only wished that my son wasn't in the same room to see his mother die. No child should ever have to see such a thing, and I wondered who would raise him in my absence. But in the silence of the room, where the only one daring to breathe was myself, I knew the answer well enough—his father. I didn't want to die, but I knew that I had welcomed death's sweet release at times, many of them spent in my alpha's bed. I hadn't thought about death so much since Gavin's birth, but I remembered those dark moments clearly, and the scars on my arms bore witness to what I'd been thinking at those times.

"You'll tell me this dream, seer," he told me, no trace of comfort in his words or tone. Someone put Gavin down on the floor near me, and tears filled my eyes as I met his wide, frightened gaze. I didn't want to tell him, but I wouldn't look in my son's eyes and wish for death either. And so I complied, giving into my alpha's commands and the momentary peace that came from obeying him.

"The pack was dead," I whispered, closing my eyes to remember the details though I wished I hadn't. He would want to know them though. He always did. "There was fire and death. Screams all around me. And so much blood. There was pain too. I don't think I was hurt, but others were."

There were whispers and frightened murmurs. I closed my eyes against them. There would be more questions for me, there always were, but that was enough for now.

chapter four

Shae

It was nearly sunset when the farmer came into the barn to find me. The wind had picked up along with the storm, coating everything outside in another thick layer of the icy stuff. The horses had started coming in, though their loud snorts told me that they wished they could go to bed without me there. I didn't blame them. The few times that I did venture into town left me feeling drained and like I'd been a fake for far too long. I'd had enough years hiding who I was and what I felt when I'd been a child. I didn't need to do that as an adult too. That was supposed to be one of the perks of growing up and getting older. I knew getting older was a form of freedom, and I relished that realization every day that I had my own mind to follow my own choices. I had consequences and sometimes what I wanted to happen simply didn't. But it was up to me, not some all-powerful man that used that shield of a title to protect himself and entitle himself to what he thought he deserved.

When the farmer joined me, I was putting up the last of the boards for the night and hadn't heard him come up behind me. Being so deep in my wayward thoughts was never a good sign and was not the safest place to be in by any means. My wolf alerted me to my own foolishness at not being more aware of what was around me, and I repeated my mantra in my head that I used whenever I was surprised by someone. 'Act human' may sound silly to someone else, someone not born of the forest and the moon, but it helped relax me. I repeated it until I knew that I had my reaction to being startled under control, until I felt safe again, and then I turned around to face him. If he'd announced his presence, I hadn't heard him, and my wolf did not like being snuck up on. I offered him a smile as if he hadn't just caused my wolf to dart forward and attempt to wrestle control of my body from me in the name of protection.

"Hey. I didn't hear you come in," I said warmly. I put down the hammer where I'd found it and forced the lid back on the coffee can of nails before pushing it away as well. I'd done a good job, I knew that. A werewolf's enhanced sight and my own attention to detail made for a pretty decent-looking barn interior.

There weren't too many women, not to mention men, who could work for as long or as hard as I did. I didn't tire like humans did, didn't get hungry or bored. But I'd had plenty of gigs like this and knew there were all kinds of people. I dreaded this part, because I knew that I'd have to accept whatever he'd want to give me for my work, even if it was lower than the discount I'd already given him when I'd come to him earlier that day.

"It's a little better," he said, his voice sounding flat and giving nothing away.

I looked around at my work, wondering how he could say such a thing. It was much improved with a good bit of the work done. But I didn't argue, only nodded and prepared to take the cash that I would be given. My wolf protested the whole ordeal. Though she didn't quite understand what had happened, she knew the value of what we had done and didn't like the feeling of apprehension in my belly. There was more work to do, not much, but we'd get by before it was time to turn in the rent at the end of the month.

"Here, thanks for stopping by." He held out a bit of money, all twenties.

I took it, easily counting it in only a second or two, and looked up at him. It was more than I'd asked for, even a little more than the amount offered on his flyer. My confusion must have been apparent on my face, because he stuffed his hands into his big flannel coat and looked almost apologetic as he said, "Sorry it's not more. You did good. But times ... they're tough, and I've got to feed my family and the livestock and ..."

I pocketed the cash. "Thanks," I said, silencing him and any further apology he wanted to give me. I didn't need it. He'd given me more than I'd expected, and I would gladly take it and give it to my landlord. Maybe he'd even let me come back and do some more work for him another time.

One of the horses loudly neighed and put his ears back. I turned fully toward him, not liking his attitude. He was trying to tell me to get out of his area. Normally I would have gladly done just that, but I was tired and my wolf was able to come closer to the surface than I would have normally let her while this close to a human. I felt my lips pull back from my teeth as if I had no control of the movement. And I likely didn't. She could be a persistent wolf when she wanted something done. I guessed I should have been glad that I was still in my skin instead of walking around on her four paws at that moment.

Although I was exhausted and really looking forward to my little bed in the cramped cottage, I fought back. It took more than I was used to giving for her to listen to me, but eventually I was back in control of my face. The human was oblivious as he went up and patted the horse on his neck.

"I wonder what spooked him, normally he's a lot calmer than this," the farmer said.

I shrugged because I thought that was what I was supposed to do as a human. I wasn't sure if it was right, but I knew that bolting out of the barn now that I had what I needed from him wouldn't have been. People would consider that rude. My wolf thought there was no further reason to hang around.

"Do you like horses?" the farmer asked me. He came away from the horse that was still watching me cautiously as if I were likely to shift and feast on him. I wanted to tell him that he had nothing to fear, at least not from me, but while I did speak wolf, and that extended a bit to dog, I had no idea how to tell him that I wasn't a threat to him. Body language could work, but I knew he likely saw me as a predator, just as I saw him through my wolf's eyes as something to eat. Something fast and big, but trapped and easily brought down in a pen full of snow and ice. The chances of my wolf getting hurt taking him down were slim, and she knew this. I could practically feel her salivating in my mind.

"They don't much like me," I told him, remembering that he'd asked me a question. I stepped back, knowing that was likely the only thing that would get the horse to calm down long enough to go to sleep later. *I'm not a threat to you*, I wanted to tell him. *I don't see you as prey.*

"Are you hungry?" he asked me, changing the subject rather abruptly, but then again the reason why his horses were so afraid of me wasn't a very good topic of discussion either. Not when my wolf was itching to get away from this place and back to our little stretch of the forest that she considered our territory.

And though I was hungry and reasonably sure that he was well-meaning with his question, I'd been around people too much already today for me to continue to be safe around them. "No, thanks," I muttered. But my words came out uncertainly, as if I didn't really know. At least my stomach hadn't started growling. Yet. Maybe we'd get lucky and find a nice fat winter squirrel to have for dinner on the way back home.

I took another step back, putting more distance between the man and myself. I was ready to go, and I felt my wolf coming awake inside of me, her restless spirit too long dormant and ready to run and play. *Soon*, I told her. *Very soon*. She was placated, for the moment, by my promise. But it wouldn't last her long. She was itching to get out of my skin, and it was time to let her free.

"Bye," I said, because it was expected of a human, and even raised my hand to wave at him like he'd waved at me when he'd seen me on his property for the first time hours earlier.

He frowned, looking indecisive as he stared at me. I kept retreating until I was out of the barn and felt the moonlight, my mother, on my face.

Subconsciously I turned toward it, and didn't realize that I'd closed my eyes until they were snapping open as the man came closer to me. I tilted my head, considering him somewhere between woman and wolf.

"Do you have a car?" He looked over my shoulder. I shook my head. "Want a ride?"

I moved my head again to tell him that, no, I wasn't interested. I felt my teeth lengthening, and my wolf pushed her way forward, growing impatient. Too long around humans and easy, penned in prey, had made her need to come out of the shell that was my body too forcefully for me to tell her no for much longer. I couldn't let him see me for what I was, what we were, and so I turned as quickly as I could manage while she fought me for control of my limbs and hurried up the hill I'd come down earlier. The forest would swallow me up as soon as I was deep enough in it. If it were summertime I wouldn't have had to go nearly as far in, but in the winter the trees were scarce and I needed the cover.

"It's negative three!" he called after me as I started running.

I didn't respond. My throat was no longer my own, but I was laughing inside of my mind. Funny; I'd thought it was colder than that. I shed my clothing as soon as I was in the forest, and by the time I was a mile beyond the man's farm, I lay naked in the snow, far more wolf than woman, despite the body that was currently on full view for every woodland creature around us.

My shift was fast, but it was hardly painless. I'd worked for a decade to make myself quick to shift. I knew the benefits of being my wolf, and she and I had long come to the same conclusion; being a wolf meant being safe. And so I'd worked as hard as I could, worked until my bones felt broken from too many shifts and I was somewhere beyond exhaustion as I lay crying on a floor after hours of moving between forms.

I tasted blood in my mouth and realized that I'd bitten my tongue during the shift. My clothing lay all around me and my wolf ignored the pieces of my human life as she trotted through the woods. I'd come back for them later. I had no control over her now, though I didn't feel betrayed by her taking over my body. We shared this soul and I welcomed her place in my life. I hadn't always, but I did now, understanding her importance. Like a shield of living body armor, she was what kept me protected, how I stayed alive. I owed her my strength and survival, and so I welcomed her place in my world.

As my wolf we ran, taking flight over freshly fallen snow and over downed and rotting logs. She was beyond fast as she trailed after prey only she could smell. With no control of our body, I was left in the background, only able to see through her eyes and distantly feel the wind on my face as if through a memory or dream. I didn't mind; this was my chance to rest, to let her have a moment to herself. She would never put us in danger, although I hadn't always had such faith in her. But at this point I knew who my wolf was and what she was capable of. And I didn't doubt her for a moment.

I listened to the sounds of the forest night as my wolf moved around. The snow crunched under her large paws. It hadn't let up during the day, and with the temperatures quickly dropping, her breath was fully visible in the moonlight as a puffed cloud formed between her lips. My wolf stopped, nearly halfway home, and tilted her head back. She didn't howl; we were too near town for that to be a good idea with how easily sound travelled in the valley between the mountains, but she looked up at the moon all the same.

The snow falling around us sucked me into a memory from my first winter in the mountains. My first time with snow. My first time with Maiki. Thinking about her wasn't necessarily painful, but it was an ache somewhere further down than just my heart, and I didn't like focusing on it for too long. But for once I let it come instead of fighting the memory and the pain that I knew would follow it. I allowed the memory to come and linger as it swirled around my mind like a white wisp of smoke. It finally settled, finding a place inside my mind and heart. I'd been ten at the time. Maiki had been younger, but not by much. I couldn't remember now, but I didn't think that Maiki was more than ten months younger than me. If that. But she had always been smaller than me, and that made her seem younger than she was. Of course, I could have been wrong about her age.

But it had been a snowy winter morning. I remembered the cold, the first bite of frost as I'd stepped out of the big farmhouse that had once been my home and later a source of remembered pain. My family had stayed there overnight, welcomed by the alpha in his home before we'd had a chance to look at the houses in town. He'd told my dad we could have our pick of them. I didn't live there long. He was dead before the little house had started to feel like home, and then my mother and I had been back in the farmhouse, continued guests of the alpha.

I hadn't worn shoes that first morning, not quite sure what cold would actually feel like as I'd come from the drastic difference of a mild Arizona fall to an early and blisteringly cold Colorado winter. I'd played, raced, jumped, and sang in the snow. That had been the first morning I'd stuck my tongue out and tasted a snowflake. I remembered that I hadn't even noticed the pain that came with the cold until I'd been snatched out up into my father's arms after dancing in the frozen flakes for nearly half an hour. I don't think I'll ever forget the fear in his eyes as he wrapped towels around my feet.

I let the memory of that day drift away with the scolding I'd received that afternoon once I'd been warmed up with some soup and hot chocolate. I wasn't a child anymore and hadn't been for a few years. Though I was considered young by most people, I hadn't felt like a child in nearly a decade. And I was free to make my own choices now. Or at least I would be if I'd been a woman and not a wolf.

The wolf stopped, seeming as if she'd been startled. Deep inside of her mind I held still, not sure what had surprised her but knowing she'd keep us safe if it was something that could be a threat to us. But then she tilted her head back, and her long tongue rolled out of her mouth. A snowflake touched her tongue and then she was done, trotting away after the scent of a rabbit that was hiding nearby. We never linked like that, not where I thought about something and then she reacted to the thoughts. But the moment seemed over, so I let it pass as a simple anomaly.

Leaves, twigs, moss of all kinds, and wild mushrooms met my wolf's bare feet. Being at peace with myself had taken years. Being at peace with the earth was simply part of our anatomy, and we both reveled in it as a simple walk turned into a game of running through the dark forest on the trail of dinner. A rabbit, too young to be much of a meal, scattered across the wolf's path. I reminded her that she had yet to eat, but she would not kill something so young simply because she could. One rabbit wasn't much of a meal for a full-grown wolf; there was no point in chasing after one that would barely be a snack. Not while a larger rabbit waited to be taken only a few yards away. The large rabbit startled before my wolf could get to it, and my wolf had been slow to chase after it.

I knew we'd both regret that loss of a meal in the morning, when my stomach cramped from being empty for far too long and I found breakfast in a bit of trout I'd smoked over the summer. But while my wolf would have preferred a fresh kill and blood-warmed meat in her belly, smoked trout was still a far better option for a meal than canned food, and we both knew it.

I let myself slide back, no longer content to fight her for control, and closed my eyes. I didn't know what my wolf thought when I slept, or if she was like me— able to realize what was going on as we switched places. She was different than me and yet we were the same. I let her have the control she needed and trusted in my belief that she'd give up our body to me again when she was ready for a rest.

~~*

Though we switched back sometime in the middle of the night and I'd gone out to get my scattered things, I'd given her back control early the next morning while it was still night. She'd nicely asked for it as the scent of an elk came around her while we were eating our breakfast of trout. She didn't want to hunt him. There was no point to it when we had no pack to feed with the kill. But she could track him and make sure he and his kind were given safe passage as they skirted the valley. It seemed odd for me, as I rode along in the back of her mind, that a predator would want to watch over a lone elk. But then I realized why as my wolf got close enough so that we could see her fully. What I'd thought was a young male was actually a healthy adult female, and heavy with the next generation. My wolf was a hunter, a predator, and she understood that animals needed to be left to reproduce, to continue on, to cover these woods in the summer and move along to lower fields in the winter.

She, unlike humans, understood the balance that was needed between letting something live and enjoying the kill, and she followed that single elk female until she was out of our territory. I assumed that the elk knew we were following her, but if she did, she never acted like it. There was no bolting, no suddenly turning and trying to kick out at us. Instead the elk had kept moving, walking as well as she could through the often deep snow drifts, until she got to the edge of our woods.

I didn't know what stopped my wolf from going further, but she halted abruptly by a shallow, iced-over river, and we watched the elk cross before my wolf turned away again. I would have thought that maybe she'd even lost interest, except that she hadn't. I knew when my wolf was bored, and this was not one of those times. No, she'd definitely stopped there on purpose, signaled by something she knew and I could only guess at. I couldn't even ask her, because she didn't think in words. Her thoughts were a jumble of images, and they mostly didn't make sense to me. So I let them pass over me like a summer breeze through my hair as I liked to sit on the lowest branch of the tall pine tree that stood as a marker in front of the hunting cabin on those warm nights. My wolf sent me thoughts of a crow, of a lamb that I assumed was nearby, of rain falling on a river. None of it made sense to me; I let them go, not even trying to hang onto any of them as she trotted through the woods, the dark paws that I could see in front of us sometimes a stark contrast to the white snow that she walked on.

I wondered if she was cold, if she could feel the ice in her paws, if it bothered her to be out here. Though our thoughts were forever connected, she didn't respond to any of my questions. I wasn't even sure if she knew how to.

A crow flew overhead and my wolf looked up at it. I watched the beating of its wings through her eyes and imagined that I could feel the wind in strong beats against my skin. Her breath came out in a fine white mist in the cold winter's night air as she watched the crow disappear into the blackness around us. She stared at the spot he'd been for a few long minutes, and I waited with bated breath, wondering what could be holding her attention, because I saw nothing. I looked through her eyes and listened with her ears, but there was nothing out of the ordinary. Noises of the forest at night were there, but they meant nothing to me. And there was no panic in the heartbeat within her chest.

I relaxed and tried to be patient until she moved again, her tongue hanging out of her mouth as she trotted on tall, lanky legs over the forest floor. My wolf was swift and nearly silent, the way I tried to be when I walked. I emulated her as often as I could. She was grace and speed, a complicated mix of predator and guardian, yet she was also surprisingly simple. My wolf existed to give balance to the part of the world we called home. When she killed, it was because she needed to. When she slept, it was because she was tired. She never took more than she was able or spent too long in one place. Being inside her was peace; giving myself over to her felt like coming home to me, a woman that had none and only had a vague idea of what the concept actually meant.

The wolf tensed and crouched, the gently falling snow clumping against her charcoal fur as she listened to the telltale noises of the animals in the forest with her. The wind whispered through the tangle of barren branches above us, calling to my wolf and begging her for a race. Her lips curled up into a smile, and her nails dug into the soft snow beneath her paws as she prepared to charge after that challenge. I could feel her excitement, her anticipation of the run.

But then a new sound broke through the quiet of the familiar forest. My wolf's ears flicked back at the unnatural noise, and I became more alert. My wolf didn't understand what it meant, but I did, and I slowly took control from the creature as I eased back into my flesh. Panting, broken, and bleeding, I lay in the snow, letting the chill beneath me ease some of the burn from my skin.

I was renewed when I got to my feet, all of my scars gone with the uncomfortable and likely unnatural ease of the shift. No one I had ever known shifted like me. It was a painful process, and I didn't think it was supposed to be that fast. The speed of it left me weakened and near exhausted. I could have likely been in better shape had I bothered to go slower. But for years I'd been going as quickly as I could, nearly making a game of it, as I forced my body to press through the change despite the pain or the blood I could taste in my mouth and that I knew would be under my fingernails. I spat, trying to get the taste off my tongue before walking away from the blood-speckled snow a few hundred yards from my cabin. I didn't know what the blood would reveal if it was found and analyzed. I wasn't nearly paranoid enough to care. I walked on wobbly legs and shivered as the icy wind whipped against my naked flesh. My breath came out in thick clouds as I panted. The ringing of my phone continued and I knew that I needed to get to it, needed to answer it, as there was only one person that had that number, and if she was calling, I knew that I'd answer. But I had to be walking first.

"You just had to take us out here again, didn't you?" I grumbled to my wolf as she settled in for a nap somewhere in the back of my mind.

My muscles were sore from the shift, but it felt good to walk on two legs again. I'd been steadily letting my wolf have more control over the past few years. We weren't near anyone, and I thought that we couldn't be in any danger, so it made sense to me to give myself up to her, to let her enjoy herself. And besides, I trusted her to protect us or hide if someone did come too close to us. But we were careful and never went too far from town. She seemed to be as wary of the humans as I was. And it didn't make sense to keep the beast inside of myself chained up when we had so much room to simply run.

The phone stopped ringing, and I held my breath, waiting for it to start up again as I walked unsteadily on human feet numbed by the icy cold. Luckily the ringing started up again, and I kept walking toward it, my strides growing longer as my muscles adjusted fully to supporting my human body again. Being inside my wolf was like seeing through a dream. I knew what was going on, for the most part, but everything was filtered through her senses, but I couldn't easily interpret them. I smelled some of what she did, but I didn't have the information that she did from the scents around us. Sounds pricked at my wolf's sensitive ears, and I didn't know what they meant. I relied on her to process everything we encountered in that form.

It was nice to have made peace with the creature after so many decades of fighting my wolf for control. I mused on this, thinking of the years that I'd wasted believing that my wolf was anything other than a friend that only wanted to protect me when she used to fight me for control. As I thought, I followed my wolf's faint trail out of the thin forest. Thankfully my phone had been put to its loudest setting, letting me hear the ring even against the sound of the wind. Though it never rang, I'd always been in the habit of keeping its volume turned up. I got to the little cabin, picked up the phone from where I'd left it on the unmade bed, and sat down on the pile of blankets.

I didn't look at the caller ID. I didn't need to, since only one person had the number. But my breath still caught at the sound of the voice on the other end of the line.

"There's a change in the air," the voice said the moment I answered.

My heart clenched and my hand dug into the worn table behind me as I fought for balance. I clung to the soft wood, needing its strength to balance me as the familiar voice worked its way through me.

"Maiki?" I whispered, the name trailing over my lips like a lover's kiss.

"The air," Maiki reminded me, her voice her voice harsh and stinging my sensitive ears. "Something's coming." There was a low growl on the other end of the phone. The sound made the hair on the back of my neck stand on end, and I shivered, glad I was nowhere near the wolf that had made it. My Maiki had probably been completely unaware of the noise herself, like I was when my wolf slipped into an everyday conversation against my will.

"Where are you?" I asked, hoping she was listening to me and not just parroting the same information about the air. I couldn't hear anyone else in the background, but I didn't put it past the wolves she lived with to be right there listening to our call. At least that was how it had been when I'd left them.

"Elderthorne. Colorado. The air. Shae. Do you feel it?" Maiki whined anxiously. It was not anything near the noise a human could make, and my breath caught as I recognized the sound. Her wolf was worried.

I prodded the sleepy creature inside my mind, asking her to rise again. My wolf came awake instantly, eager to be let out so soon after her last run. I put a stop to that. I didn't want my wolf out, merely aware. Using pictures and feelings, I tried to convey to the wolf what I needed from her, then stepped aside, hoping I'd asked her enough that she would make sense to Maiki's wolf. I could have tried to talk to Maiki's wolf, but they didn't communicate like Maiki and I did. Their language was one of sounds that we could only play at making and pictures that made little to no sense to me.

A growl bubbled up from my throat, and though I wanted to clear it after making such a noise, my wolf had other ideas as she tried to comfort the one on the other end of the line. It was difficult to communicate this way, especially for a creature that relied on touches and eye contact much more than sounds. But after a few minutes, my wolf stepped back, giving way to my mind as she settled into the darkness again and went back to sleep.

When I took the phone again, I was glad to hear no more whining from the other end of the phone. "Maiki?" I asked tentatively, hoping her wolf was calmed as well.

"Shae."

I could hear the smile in Maiki's voice, felt it like sunshine against my fur in the early spring as it chased away the cold, and it settled something inside me. "Do you need help?" I asked, keeping my voice soft, gentle. I could not risk upsetting her frail wolf with too many questions or too harsh of a tone. I knew that Maiki's alpha did that plenty on his own, and I didn't want to put in my problems on top of hers. I may not have known much about Maiki's life after I'd left her in the pack, but I knew that she didn't need that kind of stress.

There was a moment in which Maiki said nothing, and I stared across the tiny kitchen of my rented cabin until the faded blue wallpaper blended in with the pale blue of the winter sky beyond. But then Maiki spoke, and I could hear the fear behind her words.

"You need to come home. To us. Something's coming. We'll need you. He needs you."

My lips pulled back in a snarl, but I would not release that hatred on her submissive wolf. However, I knew I'd go. Not for him, though. Never for him. But for Maiki I'd always be ready to run back there, and in that moment I realized I'd never really gotten all that far. I took a deep breath to quiet my anger, then said, "I'm on my way." It was a promise, but of what I couldn't be sure. I'd go there anyway, to whatever fate awaited me.

The line went dead, and I let the phone drop to the bed beside me. I supposed that was it, then; there was nothing left to say after that.

chapter five

Maiki

"Did you call her?"

I shivered as the force of my alpha's presence washed over me. I slowly put the phone down and nodded. This wasn't right. I wasn't supposed to feel this way about him. My alpha, he was to be loved. Wasn't he? Something must have been wrong with me to have this kind of reaction in front of him. That had to be it. Everyone else loved my alpha, but I'd never been able to do so, not like I thought an alpha should be loved. I knew I had to try harder, to give him more of myself. But there were only so many fractured pieces I could give him before there were no more pieces left of myself for me for me.

"Well, what did she say? Is she coming?" my alpha asked me. He sounded impatient, and I flinched.

His hand came up to grasp my shoulder. I nodded again, my shoulders rounding as I tried to become smaller and less noticeable. Maybe then he'd forget about me. It didn't work, but then again it never did, and his hand trailed up to the back of my neck and tangled in the sensitive strands of my short blonde hair.

"Good. It'll be good to have our stray little wolf back again. Won't it?"

I couldn't lie to him. I'd never figured out how to. But he expected an answer. And I didn't have one for him. Shae had left for a reason. I knew this. And her reason was standing right next to me and his hand was in my hair. That he'd wanted me to call Shae had been a surprise. He'd forbidden it every other time I'd approached him until I'd stopped asking years before. He had her number but had to have known that Shae would never come back for him. She was the strongest wolf I knew, and from the few glimpses of her life that I'd caught in my dreams and had to tell him about, he must have known that too. Strength in numbers was the pack way; having Shae there would only help him avoid whatever was coming for us all.

I'd called her because he'd told me to. But I'd also reached out to Shae because it had been ten years since I'd last seen her and I wanted her back. It was selfish, but I did it anyway.

"Come on, seer, answer me," he coaxed. "You want your girl back. Don't you?"

I held back my sigh of relief and slowly forced my neck to make the careful, concise movements of a nod. I could answer him honestly about that. I wanted to see Shae again. I'd missed her. That wasn't a lie.

His fingers tightened in my hair, and with one yank I was forced roughly to my knees on the hard wooden floor. "Now, little wolf, tell me what you see." His voice was dark, the command behind it clear as I closed my eyes and tried to bring that other part of me in to settle down.

The woman, the wolf, and the seer in me rarely all worked well together and certainly not on command, but as his hands twisted in my hair and pain began to lace through my skull, I tried to force the connection until his deep growl against my ear halted my thoughts. It wasn't just that he'd interrupted me; it was that his presence frightened me, annoyed my wolf, and irritated the seer all at once until I didn't know which part of myself turned and looked up at him.

The only thing I was sure of was that I wasn't the one that pulled back my upper lip in a fierce display of something I should have never shown my alpha. And my reward for such behavior was a swift and painful smack across my cheek that had me falling to the floor in a heap as I played dead under him. I hid inside of my mind as the tip of his boot met with my ribs. The wolf inside of me whimpered and the seer trembled, but against the sound of her alpha's yelling, the wolf's noises meant little. There were other noises too. I could hear them from where I lay as quietly as I could, trying not to encourage him to do more to me today. Men ran forward, likely wondering what was happening in their alpha's house. But none came further than the front door. I met their gazes as blood filled my mouth and leaked over my cracked bottom lip. Another kick to my belly had me choking on the thick fluid as tears fell from me eyes.

A few of the men looked away. Some whined, their wolves wishing to help me, the weakest of them all. But they wouldn't. I'd long ago given up hope that they'd rescue me. Most of them were a few decades older than me and had been here when things had started to go so very wrong. They hadn't helped me as a child, and I knew they'd do nothing to help me now. Especially since now I'd gone and done the unthinkable. I'd brought Shae back to him. Shae was the only wolf I'd ever cared about, and now I'd lured her out of hiding. I closed my eyes and let the tears fall freely.

I cried for the child I was, broken and bleeding in a room upstairs after the first time my alpha had pulled me to him. I wept for the son I'd brought into this world, a life that had grown inside of me and that I'd sworn to protect, knowing that by letting him live I'd already likely let him down. And for Shae I shed the most tears, because as a child her only choice had been to run. I should have let her keep running, as I knew that my alpha wouldn't make the same mistake with her now that she was an adult. He'd kill her, I was sure of it. And I'd knowingly brought her to her death.

I was still crying when my alpha left me there in the kitchen with blood pooling around my mouth. My wolf had long retreated from the scene, and the seer had left me as well. In that silence, I heard him joking to the men that had stayed to watch, and I closed my eyes as, for once, they didn't take him up on his offer where I was concerned.

chapter six

Shae

It took me nearly three days to arrive at the sleepy little mountain town of Elderthorne. Though not much had changed, I took note of the differences in the trees. They helped to remind me that I'd been away. That coming back wasn't permanent. I wouldn't be staying long; just enough to make sure that Maiki was all right and hopefully convince her to leave with me this time. She'd turned me down a decade before. I hoped she wouldn't do it again today.

The wolf took a breath and placed her paw on the base of a nearly white Aspen tree, glowing against the early dawn. I wasn't a child anymore. I wasn't running away. My wolf couldn't understand this thought as she continued trotting along the side of the road. It wasn't the safest way to travel, but my wolf wanted to see the differences as much as I did. She sent me pictures of what it had been like. I didn't need them—I remembered this place too. But it helped me put together what she was thinking as she gave me an image of a house as it once was along with what it was now. She remembered the pain we'd been through here, though in a very different fashion. I remembered the words, the scars that they'd left on my mind and heart. The wolf was far more tactile and focused on the feeling of fists and feet on her fur, of teeth on her neck and the taste of blood on her tongue.

Admittedly, that last bit wasn't completely uncommon. Even now the acrid taste lingered on my lips from the rabbit I'd eaten for dinner the night before. The wolf was thankful to be let out, in her own way. It wasn't in so many words, not like I would have expressed the feeling. But it was there all the same. The wolf is faster, stronger, and far less bulky than I am. I protested, thinking about clothing and my phone, both things we'd left behind at the cabin. The wolf paid no attention to the images of human things that I sent her, things I knew I could go without but that I'd grown accustomed to. But we were here to do one thing, and after that we'd be gone again.

I sent my wolf a feeling and watched in her mind to see what she thought. It took her a moment to place it, but once she had, I knew that she felt better for having received it. I trusted her and I wanted her to know that, especially as we walked into the place where I had first learned not to trust anyone. That was why I had let my wolf out for the journey, why we were approaching on four paws and wearing fur. The wolf was safer for me, and while I was not as weak as I had been, I was hardly strong enough to take on the man who had hurt me as a child.

A blue door opened across the narrow street, and a face peeked out from the shadows. The wolf kept walking while I sought to remember and eventually did. I recalled the family that had lived in that house when I'd been just a small child playing with the other pups in the street. The man in the doorway watched us, and though I didn't know him from my short time in the pack, the wolf knew he wasn't a threat. I could feel that in her and in the way she easily dismissed him after just a cursory glance. He was submissive to her and would never be capable of doing more than watching her curiously. My wolf hurried along the road, the gravel falling away from her paws as she walked.

More people opened their doors to see me now, as if there had been an unspoken call on the morning breeze announcing my arrival back into the place I'd once called home. I heard their fevered whispers. The wolf was more interested in an elk off in the forest. Its musky scent lingered on the grass it had walked through only a few hours before. The idea of the hunt, of having a meal that large, was only a momentary distraction for her before the scent of a fox distracted her. She continued on, walking past small houses and a few shops with peeling paint that showed their age through their thick glass windows and ragged exteriors.

I tried not to let the memories of my time here enter my mind. I'd grown up here, in a way. My parents had joined the pack when I'd been only ten. Three years after that I'd been gone. A cold chill that had nothing to do with the crisp morning air seeped into my thoughts, surrounding me just as the wolves in human skin had started to. My wolf sped up, not understanding what was bothering me but wanting to get away from it all the same. She didn't understand my thoughts, my fears, my trepidation. She lived in the moment in a way I'd only ever be able to attempt.

Only there was no escaping what I was afraid of. In fact, the only thing we could do was go directly toward the source of my discomfort as my wolf trotted along a quickly narrowing street. Her hackles rose as we approached the large white farmhouse at the end of the lane as the street narrowed into a fine point that fell directly at the farmhouse's front steps. I was nearly silent in my wolf's mind as she fiercely rejected the image of the place she hadn't laid eyes on in over a decade and never thought to see again.

My wolf couldn't enter without my help, so she stood on the front porch, her ears back and her tail swaying in the light breeze as she waited. Men, women, and small children approached her from behind. Some of their scents were familiar, but when she looked over her shoulder at them, none of the faces made sense. They weren't wolves. Not right now, at least; she didn't know them as humans, but I did, and I tried not to let the faces of the people I did remember bother me.

Voices drifted down to me from inside the house. Noises that the wolf didn't understand but that I cringed at. As my discomfort grew, she bared her teeth, ready to fight off whatever threat we faced. I sent her images that I hoped were calming. But there was still something there, something in the air that had my wolf's nerves standing on end, and I was too messed up in that moment to tell her that it was going to be okay. It would have been a lie anyway, since I didn't know that for a fact. I only hoped it as a litany of reasons to run as fast as I could in the other direction swarmed through my mind.

The noises abruptly subsided and footsteps could be heard in the old farmhouse. A moment later, the front door banged open, and a girl ran out, her face covered by her hands as shrill cries fell from her lips. The crowd behind my wolf absorbed the crying girl, and my wolf focused on the new set of sounds. Heavy footsteps, the kind made by humans wearing boots, came down the stairs I could see through the partially open door. We waited impatiently as the footsteps came closer and the door opened fully.

My wolf slowly blinked up at the man. He'd aged badly since I'd last seen him, and while I could tell he'd lost none of his dominance in the years since I'd run away, he was hardly the large beast of a man I remembered him being. What little hair he had was greasy now, and his once muscular form was much less so. My wolf was unimpressed and saw no reason to pretend otherwise.

I slowly uncurled in my wolf's mind, looking out through her eyes and taking in the man fully. I remembered him differently than my wolf did. After all, what he'd done to me had been as the man and not as the nearly white wolf he hid inside. But still, I looked and noticed the differences between them. I judged him as the man he was now and not the one he had been. And I did it all through the eyes of a wolf that was far stronger than the cub I had been. Now I was faster, stronger, and far braver than I had been then. And he was just an old man who used his power and dominance to hurt and control the wolves unfortunate enough to call themselves his.

With that in mind, I steadily took control back from my wolf and slowly shifted. The wolf helped me along, something she normally wouldn't have done. But she must have somehow been able to sense that I needed her strength and that appearing weak in front of this man would never be acceptable. Old magic fused with my human form, and I found the shift far easier with the animal's help as I rose to my full height in front of him.

"Ray," I greeted him, his name dripping off my lips like the poison it was.

He smiled at me, his rotting teeth showing me even more about his lack of attention to his own health. "Shae. Darling. Won't you call me Dad?" He moved to take a step toward me, but I bared my teeth at him. It wasn't as impressive as it would have been if I'd still been a wolf, but the action meant the same thing, and it stopped him where words might not have.

"Where's Maiki?" I demanded, ignoring his request as I stared up into his glassy glaze. He paid no attention to my nudity, but then I really didn't think he would. If he was still the man I remembered, he preferred his bed partners unwilling and a lot younger than I was now. I reminded myself that I was an adult, a powerful wolf, and that I had nothing to fear from him. If only my wildly racing heart believed me.

He frowned at me. "Shae, there will be time enough for that. Come in, let's have a chat." He reached for me, tried to touch me and might have even succeeded, but I stepped to the side. I didn't move back. That was weakness. But I didn't have to let him touch me either. Not anymore.

"No. And you aren't my father. You took me in when he died, but you are not him," I hissed through my teeth. He was not my father or my alpha. He was just an old man. A hateful, mean old man, and he didn't have any more power over me. Realizing that freed something inside of me. He'd hurt me once. He wouldn't be able to do it again.

"Take me to Maiki. I will not ask you again," I demanded, my voice strong and clear across the morning air. I squared my shoulders and lifted my gaze the few inches I needed to be able to look into his eyes. I stared back at him, unblinkingly challenging him. *Not my alpha*, I reminded myself. It was a lot easier to stand up to him now that I was an adult. He wasn't a looming giant anymore. He wasn't the monster that had kept me up at night as I'd cried into my pillow, my body broken from the inside out. He was simply a man who was currently in my way and taking up my time.

His smile turned cruel, and I reached for my wolf, holding onto that bond for strength. She hadn't left me as was her usual practice when we traded off. She was still right there, ready to help if and when I needed her. I thanked her, mentally stroking my fingers through her dark fur as we waited for him to either get out of our way or to attack us.

"Seer!" Ray bellowed, sending a ripple of emotion through the gathered crowd. The humans behind me trembled, the force of his dominance spurring them into action even if they had no idea what it was that they were supposed to be doing.

As for me, I tilted my head to the side and looked up at him, wondering why it was that he no longer had any control over me. A decade away from him and every other alpha had made a great difference to me. I'd survived, living as my wolf and hunting for my meals, even as a scrawny little girl of only thirteen. It hadn't been the life of a normal teenage girl, but then again I wasn't normal. I was a wolf, and the animal and I had grown close in those years that I had given up control of my body to the beast as a matter of survival.

"Seer!" he yelled again. This time his impatience made a few of the younger and weaker wolves behind me whimper. I felt no such urge, but as he saw this, his face showing his surprise at my lack of a reaction, I smiled at him.

I took a chance and went further, baring my teeth as my wolf crouched inside my mind, ready to strike and recognizing my display for what it was and what it meant to us both. I was apparently dominant too and much more so than I'd ever believed before. The realization took me off guard, stealing my breath. He didn't control me because I wasn't weaker than him. He was a pathetic, worthless old man, and I didn't have to listen to him ever again.

chapter seven

Maiki

I heard his call and took off running, my legs stretching over the soft grass of the backyard as quickly as I could manage. I rounded the side of the house as his second call sent waves of urgency through my small frame. Ignoring everyone else, I landed heavily on the front porch at his feet, my breath coming in uneven gasps as I tried to fill my lungs.

His hand landed in my short hair, and I forced myself to hold still, to accept his touch without shrinking back. He was my alpha; this was what he demanded. I repeated the old mantra until I believed it. Only then did my breathing slow and my heart along with it. I pulled my legs under myself and knelt comfortably beside him, his boot touching my calf as I pressed myself against his leg.

"So, now that you've seen her, let's you and I get down to business."

I looked up, realizing quickly that he wasn't talking to me. My wolf recognized the woman in front of us first and the animal clawed at my mind, begging to be let out as my mouth fell open and I openly stared at the not-quite-stranger less than two feet away.

"Shae ..." I whispered on a breathy sigh. My hands balled into fists on my thighs. I could not touch her. I wouldn't. I squeezed my hands tightly together, my short nails pressing into my palms as my fingers threatened to disobey my demands.

My alpha's hands tightened in my hair, and I shrank back, my shoulders rounding as I dropped my gaze back to his boots. I had spoken out of turn. That wasn't allowed.

"Get inside," he demanded, releasing my hair.

I scrambled to my feet, desperate to obey him as I darted into the kitchen. I should make breakfast. That would keep me busy, I reasoned. But when I got to the fridge, my trembling fingers wouldn't open it. Tears splashed onto the old linoleum floor.

"Be strong," I whispered to myself. "Please." My gentle words were a desperate plea. I couldn't cry. Not now.

"Mommy. I'm hungry."

Roughly wiping at my cheeks, I turned and knelt down, opening my arms for Gavin as he stepped into the small room. He came easily, his bare feet padding across the floor and bringing him into my arms. I lifted him and sat him on the counter to better see him. "Hey, baby," I whispered, pushing his messy blond hair back from his face. "How'd you sleep?"

He shrugged and gave me a little yawn. "I heard noises again. Like—"

"I know, honey," I said, quickly cutting him off before he could voice the horrible things he'd likely heard in the night. "Daddy was working again." It was a poor excuse and hardly adequate even for a six year old. But it would have to do, because I could hardly tell him the truth.

Footsteps behind me spurred her into action, and I grabbed a juice box from the fridge and quickly handed it to him. I expected my alpha to come closer, to inspect Gavin, to tell me that he had overslept, that he needed to get dressed. But when the footsteps stopped I waited, breathing deeply and trying to calm myself.

"Oh God. Maiki ..."

My shoulders shook and I nearly lost my balance at the sound of Shae's voice. A moment later my efforts were in vain, and I crumpled to the floor, my wide gaze searching Shae's as I brought my knees to my chest and huddled against the cabinets, Gavin's bare feet swaying above me.

Shae stepped closer, her expression turning hard as she looked between us.

"Don't judge him," I whispered, hoping Shae could hear me but no one else could. I knew the others were still close. If they could hear me say that, if word got back to him ... I fiercely shook my head. That couldn't happen.

Shae's careful movements brought her in front of us, and I stared up at her, wondering what she must be thinking. After another few minutes of silence, I managed to shakily get to my feet.

"Who's that?" Gavin asked, setting his juice box aside.

I helped him down from the counter and put the box in the trash. "Mommy's friend. Hey, tell you what, go get dressed and I'll make you some breakfast. Hurry now, love."

He flashed me a smile and took off the way he'd come. When he was safely out of earshot, I turned back to Shae. "You shouldn't have come," I whispered. I didn't know how she'd got into the house, if Ray had heard her come in, or if he'd come storming in after her at any minute. People were not allowed in without his permission, and I didn't think Shae qualified for that.

Shae lifted her hand to my face. I leaned into her touch until I felt her thumb brush against a mostly healed bruise on my cheek. I pulled back instantly, but Shae boxed me in, pinning me to the counter with a hand on either side of my hips.

"Tell me he's not the father," she hissed, her voice dangerously soft. "Tell me you fell in love. That you're married. Anything but how that child has the same eyes as that man."

I shuddered and crossed my arms over my chest. I couldn't. I wouldn't lie to Shae. "My son's name is Gavin. He's mine. Mine," I repeated, hoping Shae understood. "I love him."

"And how could she not?" a cold voice called as my alpha joined us in the kitchen.

I watched as Shae appeared to shudder before she stepped away from me. I wanted to grab her hand, to pull her close, to put her between me and my alpha. But I couldn't. I didn't have the right to touch her. I was far too low to be given that gift.

"Where's breakfast?" he asked me, pulling out a chair and having a seat at the small breakfast table beside the window. Shae stepped back again, putting even more space between us. But it didn't matter. The years had already put miles between Shae and I, and a few more feet in the old house wouldn't really matter at this point. I'd lost my charcoal wolf one horrible night so many years ago, and I didn't have the right to want her back. Not anymore. Not after all that I'd done.

Closing my eyes to keep back the tears, I turned and opened the door of the fridge, wondering what I could possibly make for my alpha from the few scraps of food he'd remembered to get at the store. They had eggs, which were always better than nothing, I supposed.

"Are you staying for breakfast?" I asked Shae as I leaned my head further into the fridge. There had to be more than eggs in there. I just wasn't looking hard enough.

"Don't see that I have much of a choice. You asked me to come and so I'm here. Can't really leave until I know what's going on," Shae replied, her tone harsh. "But don't fix me anything. I won't be eating with him."

I tried not to let Shae's anger bother me. Logically I knew that her anger was completely valid. She had every right to be mad at the person that had taken her childhood away. But still there was something inside of me, something that said I should argue with her, to defend my alpha even though I had no real love for him.

"Now don't be like that, Shae. You always were such an uptight child."

I crouched in front of the open fridge, the carton of eggs trembling in my hands as a new woman joined us.

chapter eight

Shae

I closed my eyes and took a deep breath, needing that desperate moment as the familiar scent of mint and lavender came up behind me. After I centered myself, I turned, refusing to give the older woman my back as she entered the kitchen. "Diane," I greeted her, giving her no more than that as she made her way across the floor and found a seat across from Ray.

"Well, I guess it's a miracle that you're even saying that much to your poor old mother. Come. Give Mommy a kiss."

I didn't move toward her. After a moment, her wrinkled face dropped along with her outstretched arms. She hadn't changed much in the years since I'd last seen her. She'd aged, as had everyone else that was familiar in the pack. But her deceptively sweet smile hadn't.

Diane reached across the table and laid her hand on Ray's wrist. Her gold ring lit up in the morning sun. It was new and I wondered, briefly, how long it had taken her to replace the one my father had given her. She never deserved my father, and I'd hated her long before I'd come to fully realize the extent of her evil. "Ray, darling, I think I'll go pick out some clothes for my daughter. It's not right for such a pretty girl to be nude in front of all those men."

"Don't bother," I bit out, crossing one leg over the other and resting my arms behind me on the counter. If my nakedness bothered her, that was her problem. I lived alone and had become far too happy not having to listen to others to start caring about what they wanted. "I won't be wearing skin that long. As soon as Maiki tells me what she needs I'll take care of it and then I'll be gone."

She pouted, her full bottom lip sticking out so far that I could see the bright red lipstick that had been smeared onto her bottom teeth. "But you can't. I was so hoping you and I could have some mother-daughter time together. We could catch up. Talk about your life. Have you met a man?"

I laughed without warmth, and it felt good to be so spiteful as her face crumbled and her cheeks lost some of their unnatural color. "Let's stop pretending, shall we? You aren't my mother any more than that man is my father. Mothers don't force their daughters into the bed of a man four times their age. You two are strangers to me, distant memories from a past I'd like to forget. And that's all you've been for me since the day I left here."

Ray rose from the table, his chair sliding back loudly across the floor. "There's no need to be such a vicious bitch, Shae. Now, you apologize to your mother, you little brat."

I lowered my head and grinned at him, my wolf inside of me crouching against my skull and begging to be let out. "Fuck you, asshole."

He was on me quickly, his large hand grabbing my upper arm as the other made a fist at his side. I saw him raise his arm, push his shoulder back, and get ready as if each movement happened on its own, as if the act was halted halfway through and never fully realized. I pushed him back before he could strike me, unwilling to let him do so again.

The gasp that came from Diane didn't matter to the predator as my wolf looked out through my eyes, sizing up Ray advancing toward us. I rounded my shoulders, arched my back, and called to my wolf, giving her permission to be as she wanted to.

A shrill cry broke through the house, hurting her ears as her bones broke and her soft charcoal fur cascaded over my human skin. Four paws landed on the chipped linoleum where before there had only been my pale feet. The wolf shook herself, feeling right in her fur, and I smiled into her mind as I settled back to watch. Ray stopped coming at us, and his mouth fell open. Diane stared as well. The wolf licked her lips and stepped closer to him. Unafraid, her big paws brought her right up to him.

"You can't ... No one can change that fast ..." he mumbled, stepping back as she advanced on him.

I wanted to gloat, to tell him of all the long nights I'd spent picturing his face, his body above mine, and how I'd forced myself to shift over and over for hours until I'd passed out from the pain just to get it right. I wanted to tell him about how I used to time myself to make sure I was fast and then to keep going until I was even faster than that. But human words mattered little now. The wolf hunched her back, lowered her tail, and snarled at him. She didn't like him, but it wasn't the same anger that I felt toward him. She disliked him because he was someone that had tried to hurt us. I hated him because of what he'd done to me so many years ago and apparently, if Gavin was anything to go by, what he'd continued to do to Maiki.

Diane scrambled up to him, clutching at him with her long, painted nails. The wolf hesitated. She had no emotion toward her, neither good nor bad. But still, if she insisted in getting in the way, my wolf wouldn't hesitate to take her down too. I let her think, let her be, let her take the lead on this one. She understood concepts like family and mother, at least I thought she did, but there weren't enough images that I could send her that would let her know just how much I despised the woman that had given birth to me.

A scrambling noise from behind us had my wolf spinning on her big paws, ready to defend herself from an attack. But Gavin wasn't a threat. He hugged Maiki's arms as she pulled him against her chest.

"You wouldn't hurt a child, would you?" Ray's words echoed her own thoughts as he came closer. Her ears flicked back and she bared her teeth, a low growl bubbling up from deep in her throat. The sound was meant as a warning to him not to come any closer, and as his footsteps ceased, my wolf was glad to know that he'd listened.

"Of course she wouldn't. She's a good girl. Aren't you, Shae?" Diane's nasally voice did nothing to calm her feelings toward him. But the look in Maiki's eyes, that moved something inside my wolf's mind as she approached her with her head down and her tail lowered until it dragged along the ground behind us. Maiki wasn't prey, but she was still frightened as my wolf approached. The wolf could hear her heart beating in her skin-covered chest. Memories of playing with a tawny wolf in the sun floated toward her on the Maiki's scent, and she shared those images with me, knowing somehow that I'd want to see them too, to know what Maiki's smell told my wolf. They were thoughts of a childhood of happiness, one I barely remembered but that my wolf had kept safe. She sniffed the woman's hair, being careful not to touch the boy in her arms as she tried to remember more of the wolf hidden from her view.

"Come here, boy."

The wolf stepped back as Gavin began to move. He gave her an unreadable look, but there was something there in his wide, brown eyes that I took notice of while my wolf easily dismissed it. Children were strange, according to my wolf. Which was probably why she'd never had any. And living alone didn't help that either. I'd never considered a life with a child in it, and now that I knew where Maiki stood on caring for Gavin, I wasn't sure what I thought about the reality of Maiki having a child of her own.

But none of that mattered at that moment in the small, sunny kitchen as my wolf and I stared into the human eyes that hid her old friend, a small, tawny wolf, from her. My wolf touched her cold, wet nose to Maiki's cheek, wishing she had been able to press against warm brown fur instead. Her wolf was in there, somewhere beneath the frightened mask of Maiki's face. My wolf yipped, the high-pitched sound meant to draw the other wolf out as a call between friends in a pack. But when she didn't emerge, my wolf stepped back, not understanding. I tried to soothe her frustrations with the gentle stroking of fingers against her mind, but it did little to dissuade my wolf's thoughts on the matter. Her wolf was in that human body and she wanted her to come out. It was such a simple demand, yet the tawny female had made no move to obey her. I understood her impatience, her desire to play and see her mate again, but I didn't know why Maiki wasn't coming out either. It was frustrating for both of us, and I hated not having the answers I sought.

"I can't ..." Maiki whispered, shrinking back against the peeling paint of the cabinet behind her shoulder. The wolf's ears went back and her body went still. The words meant nothing to her. They were empty as far as my wolf was concerned. But the pain behind them caught her attention and wouldn't let her look away.

A chair scraped behind them, and my wolf's nose twitched. "I'm still hungry," Ray called, his heavy footsteps shaking the floor beneath the wolf's paws.

Trembling, Maiki got to her feet, her fingers clutching the ugly green countertop so forcefully that her skin turned white. "Yes sir," she said, her gaze falling to the wolf at her side.

Anger quickly overtaking her thoughts, my wolf's lips pulled back in a snarl. The tawny wolf was not there. She hadn't come out, hadn't listened to her call. Maiki with her rounded shoulders and bruised cheek had hid her. Despite my quiet protests, my wolf turned and trotted out the open front door, her big paws barely making a sound as she leapt down the stairs and landed in the soft gravel.

People watched her go; some even called to us in their own human ways. But my wolf didn't stop for them. Only the tawny wolf mattered, and she'd been lost to her, as far as my wolf was concerned.

chapter nine

Maiki

"Well, that went well," Diane said snidely as I placed a plate of toast and eggs in front of her. She picked at them, shuffling them around on her plate before pouring salt and pepper on them.

I pulled Gavin into my arms and sat him on his stool in front of his bowl of cereal.

The alpha took a bite of his eggs, made a sour face, and kept eating anyway as I sat down on the linoleum next to Gavin. "What'd you expect? She's always been a headstrong brat. Never had any sense. If she'd stayed longer, maybe I could have fixed that in her. But you let her get away." He shot Diane a dark glare.

"I didn't let her do anything," Diane snapped at him. "She ran. How the hell was I supposed to know she'd get away? If you hadn't passed out that night. If you'd actually locked her up like you were supposed to, this wouldn't have happened. She was a kid. She wasn't actually supposed to get all that far."

"Well, if you'd—"

I tuned them out, instead focusing my attention on Gavin as he quickly ate his sugary cereal. It was an old argument between them, and for as many years as I could remember, it had always ended in a draw between them, neither willing to admit they had any responsibility for Shae's escape.

I wished I could take some, though. I shouldn't have hid behind the couch, too afraid to go with Shae when she'd ran. If I had, if I'd actually trusted my wolf that night, things would have been so much different.

"Mommy. You're crying," Gavin said, reaching for me.

I quickly rubbed my eyes, wishing he hadn't seen the tears I hadn't even known I'd released. "I'm sorry, baby. Mommy just had something in her eyes. Too much pepper."

Diane rolled her eyes and scraped her fork loudly against her plate. I turned away from her and rose to take Gavin's empty bowl to the sink. "Sir?" I called, my voice trembling as my hands curled at my sides.

"What?" He didn't look up at me as he took another bite.

I shifted my weight to the side and looked toward Gavin. He was watching me too, and I smiled at him, hoping to reassure him with the simple gesture. "May I take Gavin outside? It's such a nice day and I've finished with everything, so—"

"Yes. Go on. If you see Shae, bring her back inside before I have to make her." He waved his hand at me, dismissing me from his house.

Not willing to risk him changing his mind, I reached for Gavin's hand and quickly ushered him out of the house. I didn't release my inhaled breath until the back door closed behind us. Out in the sun, I smiled fully at Gavin and lifted him into my arms, twirling him in the tall grass as he laughed and held his arms out behind him.

"I never thought you'd be a mother."

I stopped spinning and held Gavin tightly to my chest. "Hello, Shae," I said as she walked up to us.

"We should talk," Shae said once she was closer. She still stayed more than a yard away, and the distance hurt, but I tried to understand despite having no idea how to fully accomplish such a thing.

I knew that we had a lot to say to each other after so much time apart. "Yes." My voice came out weak, and I saw Shae flinch at the sound. "I'm sorry. I shouldn't have asked you here. It's not safe. It's not right. And—"

"Is there somewhere else we can go?" Shae asked, her gaze flitting to the farmhouse beside us.

Blushing, I looked away. "I'm sorry. I should have thought of that. There's somewhere close. It's a small field. Not very big, but it's private. Would that work?"

Shae tilted her head and nodded. I understood that I was supposed to lead her, but I hesitated. Gavin reached up and tugged on the short strands of my hair. Shae motioned for me to go, and that spurred me into action. Regardless of her gender, Shae was a dominant wolf, and I knew where I stood in the pack. Hesitating to follow orders again wouldn't be a wise decision, and to make up for my earlier inaction I walked faster than I normally would have along the barely noticeable trail that cut through the large back yard.

When we were safely away from the house, I put Gavin down and sank to my knees in the chilly grass. The winter sun was warm against my back as my old dress splayed around my thighs. Shae was slower to come down as I watched her scan the surrounding area.

"Mommy, can I go play?" Gavin asked, his small hand gripping mine.

I gave him a small smile. "Of course. Go have fun. But don't go too far and yell if you need anything, please."

He grinned at me before taking off as quickly as his short legs would let him go.

"He's cute, in a kid sort of way," Shae said as she came down to the grass with me.

I watched him go, making sure I knew where he was, before turning back toward Shae. My alpha would want me to bring her inside right away. And I would, soon. I just wanted a minute or two for myself. "Yeah, he is. And Shae, I'm sorry—"

Shae's amber gaze narrowed on me, and the words died on my lips. "You don't apologize to me again. Not to me."

Swallowing thickly, I dropped my gaze.

"So why am I here?" Shae leaned forward, her dark hair falling in front of her face. She brushed a hand over her cheek, pushing the long strands behind her ear.

I turned away, not wanting to be caught watching her. We weren't kids anymore, and looking meant something entirely different now than it had back then. At least to me it did. But still, I couldn't resist taking one last look at Shae's nude body. She'd always been strong, and her muscles had filled out over the years. She looked powerful and fierce in a way that was completely foreign to me.

"I had a dream," I said, my voice going soft as a warm breeze tickled the hair at the back of my neck. I could hear Gavin running nearby, his little feet crunching leaves as he played.

Shae nodded. "Bad?"

I shivered, despite the warm sun on my back. I'd known that telling Shae about the vision would be inevitable, but that didn't make the chill of it any less. "The pack died."

Shae's breath caught, and I closed my eyes. "Impossible."

I brushed some of my blonde hair away and pulled my knees up to my chest, hugging them close. "I thought so too. But then the next night I woke up from the same dream. Everything was gone. The houses were still here, but the farmhouse was burned, and then I saw the bodies. They weren't in the first dream, and Shae, they were destroyed."

"Impossible," Shae repeated.

I narrowed my eyes at her. "Saying it again doesn't erase what I saw."

Shae shook her head. "No. But sometimes you can be wrong. We both know this. You aren't always right."

"But I am about this. Every single night since that first time I've had the same dream. There are bodies in the street, the farmhouse is burning. It's just ..." I trembled, and my fingers dug into my legs. Talking about it brought all of the details to the surface, and I couldn't see them again. Not yet. I had hours before I had to go to bed and see them. I didn't need to relive it so soon.

"Do you know what causes it?" Shae asked.

Frowning, I sighed loudly. "No."

Shae pursed her lips. "Then why call me? What do you think I can do about it?"

"The alpha said to call you. He's never given me permission before. Not since I got that letter with your number in it last year. But this time he did." I knew I was rambling desperately in an attempt to fill the space. Had it really been so long since I'd seen her? More tears fell over my cheeks, and I was quick to wipe those away as well. "You're so strong, Shae. I think he wants you to protect us with him." It was my best guess, and the only thing I could think of to answer her question.

Shae's snarl was weak on her human lips, but there was no mistaking the sound for what it was. "No. Absolutely not. I will not defend him."

"But you will defend me," I whispered, knowing the truth. When Shae turned to meet my gaze, I didn't look away. "I've always been your weakness. Mated to such a low wolf, such a pitiful creature ... How could you even stand to come back? And now—"

I didn't get to finish my thought as Shae pounced on me, her larger body pinning me to the cold earth below. The first of her kisses was desperately rough, and I wasn't sure what to do as Shae rested against me.

"I've never regretted that you're my mate," Shae whispered, pulling back. My breath caught as I stared up at her. My wolf moved inside my mind, coming untangled from the web I had made for her.

My bottom lip trembled, and I looked away. "I have."

Shae went still on top of me, and her breath caught. "If you don't want me—"

I furiously shook my head. "No! Never that. Oh, Shae, never that."

Frowning down at me, Shae made a noise of impatience in her throat. "Then what?"

"You're so strong, so powerful. And I'm a hindrance to you," I said softly, choking on my tears as the truth of my words came bubbling up to the surface. That had always been the problem in our relationship. I didn't deserve her. I hadn't when we were children, and I certainly didn't now.

Shae smiled and placed a gentle kiss on my forehead. "No, you're not. And you never were." She rose up, bracing herself on her hands above my prone form. "How's your wolf?"

I frowned up at her. "My wolf?" Nodding, Shae's smile grew as I watched as her eyes changed, becoming brighter. I gasped and reached up to touch Shae's face, her brown hair tickling my wrists as it fell against my hands. With Shae's wolf looking down at me, my own wolf slowly came to life from the deep, dark place I had hidden her in. "She hasn't been out in a long time," I warned her.

Shae's smile slipped into a frown. "Why not?"

"Not allowed. The alpha doesn't want us changing. We can't," I said quickly. My wolf didn't understand why I wasn't putting more room between us so that she could shift. Now that she was awake, the animal wanted to be let out, to play with the charcoal wolf that was her mate.

"That changes right now," Shae growled. The words sounded far away to my ears. "Everyone needs to shift. Everyone. It's not a choice. It's an essential part of us. Like breathing or hunting."

I shook my head, human words failing me as my wolf clawed its way to the surface of my mind. Pain erupted at my temple, and my eyes shot open, taking in a world that was much too bright. Shae rolled off me, but she didn't go far. My wolf coming to the front of my mind happened blindingly fast, and moments later while pain continued to burn over my skin, Shae's wolf looked down at me. When my change didn't fully come even as my muscles contracted and fire shot through my veins, the charcoal-colored wolf whimpered at me. She licked my sweat-slicked face as I lay trembling against the grass in the fetal position. My breath came out in weak gasps as my fingers curled into the soft dirt. I closed my eyes, begging my shift to come and ease the pain. The wolf wanted out, she was ready, but my bones didn't remember the form and my muscles ached from disuse.

"Easy," Shae whispered, her hand warm against my shoulder.

I opened my eyes to see her kneeling over me, the wolf reflecting back in her eyes despite the form her body took. I shut my eyes tightly, unable to look at the wolf's beauty when I was still in such a weak form.

"Stop, mate, stop." Her voice was hoarse, rough from the shift and full of something even darker than that.

I forced my eyes open, unsure if I could trust what I believed. Shae bent her head and licked my temple. Her nose dragged over my cheek, then her tongue flicked out to touch my chin. "Rest, my mate," Shae said. Only it wasn't Shae talking to me. I slowly nodded and breathed deeply as Shae's wolf stared down at me.

"How?" I gasped, my mouth dry.

"Asked and woman agreed. Want talk to my mate," the wolf said.

I frowned up at her as I pulled deep, ragged breaths into my lungs. "You are. I'm Shae's mate."

The wolf shook her head, sending her brown hair flying around her face. "No. My mate. Now. We talk now. No human. My mate," the wolf demanded. "You give me her. Now." Her words ended on a growl, letting me know there would be no arguing with her. I wasn't sure how I was supposed to accomplish what the wolf wanted, but my wolf was more than ready to do whatever Shae's wanted her to. They were mates, and the bond was much deeper than I could have ever known. I slowly nodded and tried to relax, though it proved to be a difficult task with the wolf's amber gaze staring down at me expectantly.

"All right. I'm going to try to bring her up," I said as I rolled over onto my back. "But I've never had my wolf speak through me. Didn't even know it was possible. And it's weird. So just ... I don't know. Be patient, maybe?"

The wolf stared at me, but said nothing more as I tried to work out how to bring my wolf to the surface without letting her take over. It'd been years since I'd even really spoken to my wolf, and I was surprised how weak the link between us had grown.

"I'm sorry, my wolf," I whispered as tears leaked from the corners of my eyes. I'd hurt her, I could feel that now. The animal should have never been locked away. It was cruel to cage her in the darkest recesses of my mind like this. And I'd done it all on a command that should have never been given in the first place. I sobbed and quickly covered my mouth to muffle the sound. I'd done so much for him, so much more than I should have.

"I'm sorry I didn't run away with you," I whispered brokenly. The wolf blinked down at me, giving nothing away as I continued to cry. "I should have. Then maybe ... maybe this wouldn't have happened. You wouldn't be here now. He wants to hurt you. He will, too. If you let him." The wolf nodded and touched Shae's nose to my shoulder.

"You rest. Sleep. Let her out," the wolf asked, her voice much gentler this time.

I nodded, wanting to obey her. I closed my eyes, trying to do as she'd said and relax. My wolf was getting impatient as she paced through my mind, eager to get out and play with her mate in a way they hadn't done since they were children.

And then it happened, and I felt warm and safe as the wolf moved forward to take my place. I tried to speak, but nothing came out. White mist circled me, comforting me like a soft blanket, and I laid back, smiling as a sense of peace I hadn't felt in years curled over me.

"Mate," my wolf whispered. She moved forward, ducking her head to lick at Shae's jaw.

Shae nuzzled her, sniffing her hair as the wolf breathed her familiar scent in as well. "Woman weak. Much trouble."

My wolf nodded and pressed her face against Shae's neck. "Bad times. Bad man. Safe now. Mate here."

"Mate has child," Shae's wolf said, turning to look in the direction Gavin had gone.

A spark of protectiveness flared up inside my wolf, and I gasped at the unfamiliar sensation coming through our link. "My cub. Ours." My wolf nudged Shae's shoulder.

Shae's wolf nodded. "Our cub. Not food."

I grinned from within my wolf's mind. I knew that teasing tone in Shae's voice, even if those weren't her words. My wolf pounced on Shae's, pinning her to the dirt. The move was dominant, but the thought behind it was not, and Shae's wolf appeared to recognize the difference as she gave my wolf a toothy grin and licked her nose.

"My mate," she said.

My wolf nodded. "Mine too." She lay down next to Shae, the chilled grass cushioning her head as she looked at her. I stroked her in my mind, petting her in an attempt to apologize. For so much more than just not keeping the connection between us open.

"Human sad," my wolf said with a puff of air that sounded like a sigh.

"Yes. Sad women. We should go. No sad," Shae's wolf said instantly. "Come. We go now." She got to her feet and I whimpered, indecision tugging at me as my wolf rose to her knees.

"He'll hurt us. Human scared," my wolf whispered, her gaze going to the farmhouse, barely visible through the thick bushes.

Shae's wolf pulled her lips back and growled. "No. He won't find. Never find. We run. We go now," she repeated urgently. "Take cub. Go now."

My wolf nodded and slowly stood next to Shae. "I teach human to shift again. Will take time. Weak bond. But will do again. We slow without shift. Must get cub. Then go."

Shae nodded and licked my wolf on her cheek. I felt something untangle inside of me as my wolf made her decision. I hadn't been asked, but then again I wouldn't have wanted to be. My gut reaction had been to say no, to stay. It was too dangerous to leave. Leaving meant he'd come after us and find us. Things would be so much worse when he found us again. But my wolf had figured that out as well, and her decision had been the opposite of mine. She trusted Shae to protect them. And Gavin too. And so her decision had been instant. We were going, and I felt better for having let her decide for us both.

"Daddy!" a high-pitched voice squealed across the clearing. Her wolf shivered and I sat up, panic taking hold of me inside my wolf's mind.

"Cub," my wolf whispered, sounding alarmed.

Shae nodded and growled. "We get cub. Then go." She stalked forward, her arms swinging loosely at her sides as my wolf struggled to keep up. I watched, trying not to send fearful thoughts to her wolf as we approached the alpha and Gavin. When we were within a few yards of him, Shae stopped and her wolf moved in front of me, shielding me from the alpha's gaze.

"Give cub. We go now," Shae's wolf demanded.

The alpha narrowed his gaze at us, and my wolf's gaze widened as she saw his hand tighten on Gavin's collar. "No, don't hurt," I whispered. Shae reached her hand back to comfort my wolf, but it did little to calm me as I paced fretfully inside of my wolf's mind.

"What the hell have you done?" the alpha demanded, stepping closer and dragging Gavin with him. "Your eyes ... What the hell?"

Gavin twisted in his hold and I tried to go for him, but my wolf stopped me, holding me back behind Shae. There were no reassuring words, nothing but the wolf's strength and stubbornness to stop me from going to my son.

"Daddy!" Gavin cried, grabbing onto his wrist with both his hands. "Let go! Hurting me! Mommy!" He kicked out, but the alpha shook him.

"Hold still, you little brat!" he snarled down at him.

Gavin went quiet for a moment before his loud wail split the silence of the clearing. Big, fat tears streaked down his face and the sight of my child crying broke my wolf's hold on my mind. My consciousness rushed forward, and I stumbled around Shae's legs, motions jerky as I reached for Gavin.

"Leave him alone!" I cried, going for him.

Before I could reach him, the alpha brought his fist down on my cheek, sending me sprawling to the ground as pain split my face. I sobbed, covering my bleeding face with my hand as I reached for Gavin. His little fingers went out for me too, nearly touching me.

A fierce growl added to my cries, and I looked away from Gavin for a moment to see a large charcoal-colored wolf standing over us. The wolf stepped closer, her ears back, her teeth bared.

"Fucking bitch. I'll teach you to growl at me," the alpha snarled at her.

He tossed Gavin to the side, but I grabbed him, bracing his fall as I pulled him into my arms and hugged my body around him. I trembled as I waited for the yelling I knew would come. My mate needed me, and all I could do was shake as I held my son. I really wasn't worthy of her. At all. I buried my face in Gavin's bright blond hair and held him tightly as I waited for the confrontation to be over. The alpha needed Shae. He wouldn't really hurt her. He couldn't. He wasn't strong enough without her, and there was something coming. I didn't know what it was, but I remembered the look in his eyes, the way he'd seemed when I'd told him. And I knew he was afraid too. And though it was horrible, the knowledge that he needed Shae and wouldn't hurt her because of that very reason was the one thing I had hope for. I wished I could ask for more than that, but there was no way the alpha would allow her to get away completely unharmed.

I sobbed. I was a horrible mate. I knew this. Of course I was. I couldn't even bear to watch my mate be hurt by my alpha. If I were a good mate, if I were a strong wolf like Shae was, I would have been right there with her. I would have been able to shift. I would have left with her all those years ago. But, I realized with a shaking breath, if I had left when Shae had first asked me, I wouldn't have Gavin, and the precious little boy in my arms was someone that I loved dearly. Despite the events of his conception and birth, neither of which he had any fault in. I kissed his forehead and chanced opening my eyes, wondering at the silence that had fallen over the big back yard.

The dark gray wolf stood motionless in the middle of the yard, the alpha a few yards away from her, his body bent and crooked as he tried to shift. I felt his urgency, his call in my blood, but I refused the cry. Others would come. I was sure of it. And Shae must know that as well. But then why wasn't she attacking him now? He was weak as a human. As a shifting beast he was even more vulnerable. Why wasn't Shae going after him now?

"Kill him," I hissed, hoping she could hear me. "Kill him now!" She didn't seem like she could hear me though, though. Shae continued to stand there, watching the alpha's change until it was complete and a shiny white wolf lay on the grass, trembling at her feet. Only then did Shae move back, giving him more room.

I saw them come before Shae did. Men, women, and children began arriving all around them, circling them. I sat up and held Gavin against my chest, unwilling to let him see what was about to happen. Especially since I had no idea what was going to. But whatever it was, the whole pack had gathered to witness it. I closed my eyes, unsure if I wanted to see a fight between my mate and my alpha. But in the end I knew that I had to watch, even if it was just to be a witness to what was about to happen. Shae deserved that much. She had attacked him to defend me, after all. I owed her my attention for that act at the very least.

The alpha circled her, his head down and his teeth bared. Still, Shae didn't move. I frowned at her, wondering what she was waiting for. Had she lost her nerve? Had she given up? What was going on?

But then the alpha lunged at her, going for her front ankle and missing as Shae side-stepped him with a growl. She attacked him then, and the attack must have caught him by surprise because his much larger wolf was forced onto his back instantly. But her success didn't last long. She was pushed back off of him and tumbled into the dirt a few feet away. Shae got up quickly, though, much faster than he did, and she was back on him within the span of a heartbeat, her mouth open and her teeth bared for his throat.

I forced myself to watch, to ignore the men behind me as the wolves tumbled together in a mess of dust and snapping teeth. Dark blood matted the alpha's white fur, and I looked to see if Shae had been hurt as well, but her coat was much too dark to tell. Gasps broke the silence of the gathered crowd, but no one moved forward to help on either side. I was glad that none of the men jumped in to help the alpha, but I wished someone would help Shae. I started to understand why not, though, why no one would or could. This was honorable, though I hadn't seen something that resembled that description for many years. Not since Shae's father had lost his life in a fight much the same as this one. I tried not to think about that, not of his cries as the alpha had torn into him or his blood as it soaked into the ground. Shae needed me to be here, in this moment. And I would do my best to make sure I stayed that way. For Shae.

Sharp cries split the air and forced my attention back onto the battling wolves. My heart in my throat and my unspent breath burning my lungs, I watched as the dust settled around them and the alpha stepped back. I shook my head, disbelieving my eyes as the white wolf stumbled but remained on his feet while the dark gray wolf lay motionless on the ground. The alpha fell as well, not more than three feet from where he'd emerged from the fight. While others moved forward, their steps tentative as if they were unsure of their movements, I could only continue to stare at the prone figure of the dark wolf. Until suddenly, unbelievingly, she rose unsteadily to her feet. I could see her shaking from across the yard, her legs threatening to give way even as she forced herself to get up on them.

Shae tilted her head back, her shiny black nose pointing toward the darkening sky, and howled. Her cry fell over the pack, its hollow sound settling in their chests, and then they moved toward her. She howled again, a cry to the others that had remained at the outskirts while she'd fought the alpha. I added my voice as well, my mate's call spurring me out of my silence as I rose to my feet. My human throat was incapable of making the call I wanted, but the meaning was the same as I carried a wide-eyed Gavin to the dark wolf's side.

I placed my hand on the wolf's shoulder, my fingers sinking into her thick fur. Gavin reached for her as well, his hand going to her ear. I tried not to see the blood on her dark fur or the way she wouldn't leave her front paw on the ground for long. Instead I focused on the brightness of her amber eyes, the strength in her gaze, and I smiled down at that familiar dark face.

"Thank you," I whispered.

The wolf licked my fingertips and turned her focus toward a sound. I looked as well, my breath catching as the white wolf lifted his head and tried to rise up.

"I thought he was dead," I hissed, my fingers tightening on Shae's fur as anxious fear crashed through me.

The wolf nodded and threw her head back to release another howl. This time it was a series of shorter noises, though the effect was no less powerful. It was a call to action, and as Shae's fur faded to be replaced by soft skin, I began to understand. She rose to her feet and circled an arm around my waist. I kissed Shae's shoulder and rested my head against her warmth.

"I've left him alive," Shae called out to the gathered pack. "Those of you that want to take your revenge, do so now. If you do not wish to kill him then I will, but I thought it fair to give you all a chance to take what is rightfully yours. You have my blessing to do with him as you wish."

I turned and watched as girls began coming forward. Most no older than I was but many quite a few years younger. They were all his victims. Shae was right; I knew they had a claim to his life. Just as I did. And the debt would be settled with his death.

"Do you want to?" Shae asked, her voice soft against my temple. "I'll hold him if you want to go over there." The first blow came across the alpha's nose, and I watched as blood poured from that broken protrusion.

I shook my head. "No. I witnessed his defeat, and his death will start to heal my hurts. I don't need to touch him again."

Nodding, Shae pulled me closer. "I understand. What are they doing?"

I turned to look in the direction of Shae's gaze and frowned as well. Men had formed a crowd beside us and, as we watched, they fell to their knees. Young and old, fathers and brothers, they all got down on their knees in front of us. My frown deepened, as I was unsure of what to make of such a gesture. The crowd of young women and girls moved back, many of them sporting the bloody evidence of their actions as they joined the men. They knelt as well, though they were smiling, in sharp contrast to the somber expressions of the men. I understood their need to smile, to express happiness even as it meant the death of someone else. It wasn't glee that I felt, but it wasn't far off. The alpha's reign was over. They'd burn his body at sunset, as was our tradition, and the girls would never have to fear another such ruler ever again. The relief floating through the small pack was nearly palatable, and I breathed it in deeply, wanting to hold onto it for as long as I could.

"Shae, we're yours, command us as you would," an older man spoke up, though he didn't move from his position on his knees.

My breath caught, and Shae had stopped breathing beside me as well. "What?" Shae asked him.

There was a murmur of confusion between them as the man looked around at the others. "You've slain the alpha ... you're the new alpha."

Shae shook her head. "No, I'm not. I'm going back to my little cabin with my mate and our cub."

"But—but that's how it works," another man protested.

Snorting, Shae shook her head again. "Well, that's just too damn bad. I don't want to do it. Not at all. You're just going to have to find someone else," she protested.

A slow smile came to my lips. "This is it," I whispered. "This is my dream. All of it. You're the thing that he was afraid of." Laughing, I rounded on Shae to better look in her amber eyes. "You destroyed the pack."

Shae frowned. "No I didn't. Not even close. They're still there. They're just not going to have me as an alpha, because I refuse."

"You can't, though," a woman called from somewhere in the pack. "There's no one else. We need you, Shae."

"See?" I said, reaching up to cup her cheek in my palm. "You are the alpha of the Elderthorne pack. You're ours. And I'm your mate. You brought death to him and killed his reign. It all makes sense. My dreams come true, and you just made it happen."

Shae's eyes widened and she took a step back, stumbling. "I don't want to be the alpha," she protested, her voice weak. "Is there really no one else?"

I looked around at the others, searching for anyone with Shae's strength, her will. Finally, I shook my head and shifted Gavin to my hip. "No one else is a strong as you. You must do it."

Though she still looked reserved, a quiet nod of acceptance had many of the women grinning as they rose to their feet and approached their new alpha. They touched her, pressed against her, and made small noises in their throats of acceptance before moving on. The men came next, and though they were quieter about their admiration for their new alpha, the evidence of their thanks was no less there in the way they approached her.

"But what about the house?" Shae asked when the last man had left and she and I were left alone with Gavin.

I nodded and turned toward the old building. "What would you have done with it?"

"Burn it," was Shae's instant reply.

"Then that's the last of my dream. The last piece fit into place. I'll make sure it's done tonight when they burn his body," I said, a sense of calm purpose settling in my bones.

Shae turned toward me, wrapped her arms around my waist, and pulled me close. "Thank you, mate."

I smiled up at her and placed a gentle kiss on her chin.

"Take your hands off me!"

With a sigh, I turned to see what the newest interruption was. My eyes widened at the sight of two of the men dragging Diane closer. "We caught her loading up one of the cars," the man on her right said. They pushed her forward, forcing her to her knees. "What do you want done with her?"

Shae didn't move out of my hold. "Diane, you're banished. Take any of the pack that is still loyal to Ray and get off my mountain. Come back again, and I'll kill you myself."

"Might be better just to kill her now," one of the men offered.

Smiling, Shae nodded. "Probably. But I think we've had enough bloodshed for one night. Let her take those who believed in Ray's ways with her. I don't want them in my pack. Spread the word that they're allowed to leave unharmed but make sure everyone knows that if they come back that they're going to die."

The men nodded and released her.

"Oh, thank you, Shae. You were always so merciful, so nice, so—"

"You've got until I count to ten to get out of Elderthone," Shae interrupted her. Diane hesitated, her mouth falling open. When she didn't immediately get to her feet, Shae started counting. "One ... two ..."

I turned away as Diane got to her feet and ran across the grass as fast as she could. Some would leave with her. Probably quite a few. But the pack would be better without them in it. The women would be safer, the men would be protected. And Gavin could grow up as he was meant to. I smiled up at Shae and breathed deeply of the warm afternoon breeze that circled around my body. I couldn't have known what my dream would bring to the pack, but now that I'd seen the darkest of it played out, I could honestly say that it was the best vision of my life.

chapter ten

Shae

The smoke finally cleared as I lay near the trees with the black sky above me and Maiki by my side on the cool grass. The cub lay nearby, blankets wrapped around him as he softly snored. He was close enough to be safe but not so close that Maiki and I couldn't avoid being heard if we were quiet enough. I hated who his father had been, but he was still my mate's child. And I would have to find it within myself to tolerate Ray's continued existence in my pack through the child that bore his eyes. It wouldn't be easy, but I would have to make it work. For Maiki I would do that and so much more than ever before. I'd let her down once by not insisting that she come with me on that terrible night. I knew that now. And I would not be making that same mistake again. I'd die before that happened.

My wolf came awake, alerting me to the change in the woods off to the left of them before I ever heard the men approaching. It gave me the extra minute I needed to wake Maiki from her deep slumber beside me. Maiki went to the cub, and I moved in front of her. I was tense, every muscle in my body poised to react as I got my first whiff of a fresh kill on the night breeze. The cub and Maiki spoke in soft tones behind me. He sounded worried. On the insistence of the whining wolf in my mind, I reached back and briefly touched him, offering my comfort to him as well as to Maiki. Though my actions didn't silence him, at least he grew quieter in his muffled worry.

I let go of him to step forward and greet the five men coming toward us. I forced myself to shift quickly, welcoming my wolf and letting her out to what I hoped wouldn't be more fighting. But I wanted to be ready for it if there was. They were dragging something on the ground behind them, and though my nose immediately told me it was a buck, it took me another moment or two for my eyes to adjust well enough to see the dead animal. I moved closer, trying not to become distracted by the smell of the fresh kill and intercepting them before they could come within distance of hurting Maiki or the cub in her arms. I didn't stand much of a chance against that many adult men, but by fighting them I could give Maiki a better chance to run. When I met them, however, they dropped the carcass to the ground at my paws before moving back several yards and falling to their knees in the grass.

I moved forward and took a big bite. The fur on my face was smeared with blood and the meat of the fresh kill quickly filled my belly, but I worked further into it until my paws were also covered in the thick, sticky blood. I was only satisfied when I had my prize between my teeth. The deer's heart was big enough to be a meal all on its own; though I didn't understand, my wolf knew to take that best part for myself. I carried it over to Maiki, who was sitting on the grass and pulling parts of the meat off for Gavin.

Once I had my piece secured, I tossed my head back and let out a long, low cry into the night sky, calling the pack around me to come to dinner. They came on foot, looking uncertain as the men that had brought the buck down started eating. There was some semblance of order, though it was a lot less defined than I would have preferred it, but while the human was lazily relaxing in the back of her mind, my wolf kept a careful watch on each of the people as they ate. There would be no fights on her watch. When it looked like something would break out between a pair of teenagers fighting over a piece of the buck's liver, I got to my feet and growled sharply at them both. Order quickly came back over the feast, and soon the heart was gone and my wolf was left licking the blood off her mate's hands as the people slowly ate their fill.

If they'd been wolves, there would have been hardly any waste. I intended to change that as soon as possible. I refused to be alpha to a group of humans. The crowd slowly dissipated, and I shifted back into my human form. The wolf was full and ready to relax while I wanted to rinse the blood off. It was a fair trade. Silently, I took Malki's hand and brought her and her son down to the stream. Even if the house had still been standing, I wouldn't have gone back in there to get cleaned up. I'd spent far too many nights cleaning blood off myself in the upstairs bedroom.

Now what had stood as a reminder of the pain of my youth only that morning was little more than a pile of rubble. The smoke had cleared, but it would take work to get the remaining pieces of the house that hadn't been willing to burn down out and away from the site. I didn't know what they'd put there, but it was winter in the Colorado mountains and they'd need to find a home to sleep in. Fortunately I held nothing against the ones that had been abandoned by the men that left with the woman that had once been my mother. They'd sleep there when the cold came back around the high face of the mountain above them. For now I wouldn't worry about it.

I stepped into the river, its icy chill making me gasp, and I smiled as I began to clean myself. Leaving Gavin on the sandy bank, Maiki joined me in the shallow part of the river, washing the blood from her arms and face as well. Once I was clean, I looked to Gavin and, seeing that he had grown a bit dirty too, reached to clean him off. But he backed away from me, his eyes wide.

"I won't hurt you," I promised him, the words sounding foreign to lips that weren't used to speaking to people, especially not children. My wolf wanted to whine at him, wanted to put her ears back and her tail between her legs as she crawled on her belly toward him. Showing that she wasn't dangerous would have been best. But after such a recent shift I wasn't about to do it again, and so I knelt down in front of him and offered him my hand, palm up. Maiki came out of the water behind me and placed a hand on my bare shoulder.

"Gavin will come around. He doesn't much like strangers," Maiki said before I could say anything to him.

I nodded, quickly realizing this. I'd make an effort, for Maiki, but my feelings about him were flat. I didn't particularly like children, and this one was fathered by someone I had considered to be made of pure evil from the first time he'd touched me. But, I forced myself to remember, this Gavin was Maiki's son as well, just as I was my father's daughter more than I would ever claim to be Diane's. Sweet Maiki may have been able to temper his father's personality with her own. It was a long shot, I was sure, but it was something I had to believe. I didn't like that my thoughts lead me to thinking that such a tiny child would be evil in any way and attempted to dismiss the thought from my mind completely. I would not judge him on his father's actions and hoped that he was young enough to be taught better.

I stepped around him and stretched my arms over my head, working out the uncomfortable knots in my spine. "We'll sleep in one of the abandoned homes for tonight," I told Maiki.

"What will you do with the pack?" Maiki asked me as she took Gavin's hand and started to follow me back to the homes.

I shrugged. I wasn't really sure what I was doing with the rest of them. I'd never expected this, never wanted a pack of my own. And so I'd never put that much thought into it. "I suppose," I quietly began, "that I'll be expected to rebuild it." My heart wasn't in it, though. With all of my memories here, I didn't want to be anywhere near this place. I wished that I could take Maiki and Gavin and leave this place. It would be so much simpler, it would mean so much less pain than standing in the middle of a tiny town that I'd spent three horrible years of my life in. As a child I'd hated nearly every minute that I'd been stuck here. Now, as a woman, I couldn't believe I was considering staying.

I went to the nearest empty house and pushed in the front door. It was a small cabin, larger than my hunting cabin but only possibly a third of the size of the farmhouse. I'd been glad to see it burn. Aside from seeing a tornado tear through it, a fire was the second best possibility. I'd wanted to see it burn for years, and while there had been joy in seeing it reduced to a smoldering pile of ashes, it wasn't nearly as fulfilling as I'd wanted it to be. There were still too many wounds, too much pain, to simply let it all go.

"What are you thinking about?" Maiki said as she released Gavin's hand long enough to go clean up the haphazardly left kitchen.

I didn't have a good answer. "Too many thoughts," I said honestly. I closed the door behind myself and tossed the nearest framed picture, one of a man and his family, into the trash near where Maiki was working.

"Why'd you do that?" Maiki asked her after she'd jumped in shock.

"They left with her, which means that I do not want their reminders around me. Too much was left to happen here, too much pain," I told her. There was no one else in the house, but I could see and feel the reminders of the family all around us.

Maiki nodded and knelt in front of Gavin. "Go find a room for yourself. Be careful, though," she told him. I watched him go, his short legs helping to carry him through the small house. He couldn't get far, and I found myself wondering at the protective warmth that flowed through me as I listened to him moving throughout the different rooms.

"I know this isn't what you expected when you came here," Maiki said in her barely-there voice as she took my hand. I squeezed her fingers briefly between mine. I hadn't known what to expect, or really what she might be referring to, and my mind was a jumble of thoughts anyway. But I could see what she meant. She looked apologetic, like a child I'd seen stealing candy from a grocery store once after getting caught by his mother. I'd watched, curious and a bit hesitant as well, as the child was scolded. He cried, but the blows I'd expected from the mother never came. I'd learned then that some parents didn't treat their children as the woman that had given birth to me had. It was a relief to know my circumstances were likely an anomaly.

I brought Miaki to the only couch in the living room, a strange, dilapidated plaid thing that was hardly comfortable but would suit my needs just fine as I pulled her to sit down beside me. But as soon as I was seated, she went to the floor at my feet. "What are you doing?" I asked her as I stared at the top of her head. She wasn't looking at me anymore, and that bothered me more than the submissive place she'd taken beside my legs.

"I'm not allowed, it's not right, I'm not—"

Silently I reached down, hooked my hand under her arm, and lifted her up to her feet. She got back onto the couch but didn't look at all at ease about it. I realized I had quite a bit of work to do if she was going to understand what I wanted from her now. "You aren't my submissive," I said gently, hoping that the words sunk in.

"Yes, I am," Maiki instantly argued with me.

I sighed, exhausted from the day and already tired of this little dance. I'd been alone too long, I figured. Too many years without a pack and now I had no use for the structure of one. "Not to me you're not," I tried again. She didn't look convinced, and I struggled with a way to make my Maiki, the one that I remembered from my childhood, understand that she was far more than the beaten woman I saw in front of me. But after a few minutes of silence, I didn't know how; I turned to face her on the couch and brought my knee up so that I could rest my chin on it while the other came under me. "I don't want a pack," I said again, wondering what I was supposed to do with them all.

Maiki nodded and put some of her blonde hair behind her ear. It was short and ragged in a way I didn't remember it being. "I'm sor—"

I growled before I realized what I was doing, and she instantly shut up, her face pinching as she turned away from me, hiding herself from my gaze. I closed my eyes and wondered what my purpose here was. I wanted Maiki and Gavin to come with me. I wanted to leave these people here to fend for themselves. They could elect a new alpha or perish in the harsh Colorado winter that I could smell coming. I really didn't care either way as long as my Maiki was safe.

"You have a duty to these people," she finally said.

I quickly shook my head. I didn't, not at all. "I have one to you, to my mate. And I failed you once already. Beyond you and Gavin, I have nothing for these people." I was adamant on that point. I didn't know these people and didn't want to start.

Her chin tilted toward me slightly. "Is that what you think happened? That you failed me?"

"Yes," I answered her, the answer seeming obvious to me. "I was supposed to protect you, my mate. I didn't."

"You were a child," she reminded me, her voice soft as she turned toward me.

Nodding, I agreed with her. "But so were you. And I've always been stronger than you. I should have done more to keep you safe. When you said no, that you wanted to stay, I should have picked you up and carried you out."

Her mouth cracked into a small smile, and I shared the expression. "You would have been slower with me on your back. The only reason you were able to get away was because you were alone and you were fast. They searched for you all night. Then in the morning—" Her voice abruptly cut off, and I reached forward to take her hand in mine, giving her a gentle squeeze. I both hoped that she would continue and dreaded what she would say to me. Had she been hurt because I'd run? Had Ray taken it out on her? But she simply shook her head, letting me know that was the end of it. I didn't push her on it, either.

I heard Gavin moving around in a nearby room and got up to go see him. I didn't know why; curiosity maybe, or something else. But seconds later I was sitting next to him and watching him play with a baseball. He rolled it back and forth across the floor between his little hands. "Hi," I said, close enough to touch him but not about to in case he shied away from me again.

"Hi."

That was good, I supposed. Maiki touched the back of my hair. I'd heard her get up from the couch too but didn't know where she was heading when she got up. I was glad to know she'd come to join me. On a whim, I let my wolf come forward when she asked gently. She stopped before doing a full shift, instead simply taking over my body as she looked at the little boy next to us. "Little cub," she said. I wondered what she saw when she looked at him, if she had the same strange sense of protectiveness that I did. Was it because he was weaker than us and we naturally wanted to take care of those that were? I hadn't experienced that with her before, but I supposed that might have been because we'd so rarely been around other people and none of them had been wolves.

She looked straight up at Maiki, and I was glad to see a lack of surprise on her face when the wolf looked at her. "Mate come out. Now." The command was so simple, so easy, as if Maiki hadn't shown us both that she was having trouble with it only a few hours before. I touched my wolf, comforting her for what I knew would be Maiki's answer. Her mate couldn't be there, not right now, at least, and though it was unfair that I had my mate and she did not, I didn't know what to say to her. My wolf knew that Maiki was ours long before I did and years before I'd even been able to shift. It was knowledge outside of myself, something I couldn't comprehend, but I remember the moment I knew. I was ten and a boy was trying to hold her hand on the street. I pushed him out of the way and took Maiki's hand myself. *She's mine*, I remember telling him. *Not for you.*

Maiki shook her head. "I can't. I'm sorry." I saw tears in her eyes and gave my wolf a shove, annoyed at her for pressing Maiki so soon when she'd already told us that she couldn't do it.

My wolf ignored me. "Try. Try now. Just us. I'm here. Protect mate."

I thought for sure that Maiki would say no again, but instead she stepped around me and knelt in front of me. Gavin went still at my side, maybe realizing how important this was to us. Maybe simply curious about us as much as I had been to see what he was doing in the abandoned bedroom. "Lie down," my wolf said, her command firm as she patted the floor in front of her. Maiki complied, and my wolf made her comfortable with her head on my lap.

"You stay?" my wolf asked Gavin. Though, even if I thought it was a question, I wasn't entirely sure that it was. My wolf often gave commands without actually considering those around her. She simply expected people to follow her directions, I supposed. Maybe having only me around to command for the last ten years had gone to her head.

"I'm scared," Gavin said, his voice as quiet as Maiki's often was.

My wolf smiled at him. "You safe here. Mother here." I'd thought she was going to touch Maiki when she told him that. Instead she touched her own chest, indicating herself, and I was left wondering what the hell had just happened. Maiki had tears in her eyes as she stared up at my wolf, and Gavin looked shocked as well. Did my wolf really mean that? Had she really just accepted Gavin so easily?

If I'd had control of my body right then, I would have been as speechless as Maiki. Instead I was only left staring out through my wolf's eyes and trying to make sense of her words. She'd never expressed ideas like mother and family before. It was always just us. But as I stared into Gavin's little face, I could see why my wolf would want to protect him. His eyes couldn't be helped, and there was so much of Maiki in him that I was starting to notice. "Good cub," my wolf said, briefly touching her cheek against his forehead. He reached up to touch us too, and I could nearly feel his touch against the hand my wolf controlled. He pulled away before she could hold his hand, but that brief contact was enough for the wolf. I could feel it inside of her. She was satisfied with him right then. I didn't blame her for caring about him. I was starting to feel that way too. But I nudged her back to Maiki, reminding her that she needed attention too.

My wolf put hands on either side of Maiki's face and hunched over her. I wanted to see what was happening, but my wolf closed her eyes and I was left in the dark as something warm swirled around us. I could hear Maiki softly crying and banged on my wolf's mind, demanding to be told what was going on, to be able to comfort my mate. She did not get to have hers at the expense of mine, I reminded her darkly. But my wolf ignored me, brushing off my cries as if I were completely inconsequential to her.

I kept yelling at her until she finally opened her eyes, and I looked down at Maiki's face. She looked shaken up, but my wolf tried to comfort me as best she could while stroking Maiki's hair. I stared, hoping for the best, as Maiki's eyes slowly changed and her body shuddered. The slow tremble continued until she shook violently, and I could only hold my breath as I watched her bones slowly break and her mouth open on a silent cry. It was excruciating, and if I'd been able to cry I would have been as I screamed like Gavin was doing, only my screams were silent inside the wolf's mind. But minutes later a small, tawny wolf lay against our legs, and my wolf fully took over my body as she shifted as well, and I was pushed into the furthest recesses of her mind.

As I was wrapped in a warm mist, she lay down next to her mate and licked the tawny wolf's face before putting a paw on Gavin's leg. He came closer, putting his arms around the tawny wolf's neck and lying between them in the abandoned bedroom. I momentarily wondered at the safety of him between the two wolves, but I quickly realized that I needn't have bothered as they both licked at him until he was giggling between what I knew from his perspective had to be two massive wolves. In reality, I knew that we were about the size of a regular wolf, maybe even a little smaller.

chapter eleven

Maiki

I wasn't back in my own skin until just after sunrise the next morning, and though I'd spent my first night as a wolf in years I wasn't quite ready to leave her gentle embrace. My wolf was comforting and warm. I reluctantly came back to myself and stretched out beside Gavin and Shae, who were still asleep. My dress lay in tatters around me, but for once I didn't care that I was naked in Elderthorne. I wasn't vulnerable like this. Not anymore.

Getting to my feet, I went outside to greet the new day. I saw others doing the same, many of them without clothes as well. When a young girl smiled at me, I smiled back at her, surprised to see such emotion from one of the girls that had most certainly been a victim of Ray's. I wandered around the town for a bit, catching gazes and nodding at those who nodded at me first. I was used to being nearly invisible in this pack but found that I didn't mind the attention now.

My wolf was a constant presence in my mind, a familiar friend that had left with a nearly audible promise to come back as soon as I needed her to. I didn't doubt her promise. I'd felt her the previous night, and she'd blocked most of the pain of the shift.

I knew this because I could feel the pain, dulled through the shield she'd become, but it was most certainly there like sandpaper against my skin. It was if I were outside of myself, understanding that bones were breaking but not that they were necessarily mine. And I was grateful for her taking that darkness of the experience from me. I wished that I could speak with her, to share in her wisdom and tell her how grateful, and especially how sorry, I was. But my words had little meaning for her, at least from what I could tell.

I found myself kneeling by the river and splashing the icy water over my face. Leaves rustled behind me and my heart began to race, but my wolf worked to calm me as instantly as the fear had come. I was safe; I could tell that by our connection. Just not in so many words. It was more of a feeling, a knowing that nothing in this world could hurt me again. Because she was there for me, and Shae was with us now as well. Shae to me, the dark wolf to mine. They had no names, only feelings. I turned to look over my shoulder as a small, reddish wolf crept closer. It had been so long since I'd seen any of us shifted that I did not recognize this werewolf, but I knew they weren't a threat to me as they crouched at the water and took a drink beside me. When they were done, they laid down beside me, their stiff fur brushing against my thigh. They weren't asleep but they hardly moved, and I didn't have the heart to tell them to go away.

Slowly more wolves began to join us by the river as if somehow called. Some drank; some simply lay down around me. I didn't know what was going on, but I didn't move, too afraid that they would scatter as unexpectedly as they'd arrived. Shae's wolf joined me an hour later with Gavin perched on her back as if she were a pony. He slid off when she got close, and I was surprised to see the wolves around us make a path as she approached me. There was no noise, no fighting, just the simple movement of a group of werewolves parting as if in a wave to make room for their alpha. Seeing this, how they all reacted to her and respected her, I couldn't believe Shae still didn't see her place here on this mountain. With all of us.

I touched the fur on her face and took Gavin into my arms. Shae was there somewhere within the wolf's mind, but the animal in front of me was part of her too, just as her mate was part of me. "Hello," I told her, wishing that we didn't have an audience as I wanted to say everything that I was feeling, every little thought that was currently running through my head at a wildly galloping pace. I wanted to thank her for holding me through my first shift in years, for coming back to me, for accepting Gavin into her life, for bringing my own wolf back from whatever dark hole I'd put her in.

This wolf needed to know all of this and so much more, and I hoped that she did, or at least could someday. "Do you see us now? How much we need you? How you couldn't be anything but our alpha?" I whispered to her, knowing that the wolf could hear me and that Shae was likely listening as well as I cupped my hands on her dark gray cheeks. We needed her, all of us, but me most of all. Shae was my mate, and I'd gone too many years without having her by my side. I'd do whatever she needed me to, pay whatever price she asked, if she just remembered that simple fact. This was my mate, she was my family, and she was needed here.

My Shae slowly emerged from the wolf in an impossibly fast shift that left her breathless and me aching for the pain she must have been through. My hands slipped to her shoulders, and Shae looked up at me, her amber eyes wet. "Don't you see though, Maiki, that there are too many memories here? And, even if there weren't, I'm not alpha material. I don't know how. I don't know the first thing about taking care of someone else. I've never had to."

The people around us began to shift as well. Those closest, anyway. The outer circle remained as wolves as they stood watching us. I had the idea that they were somehow protecting us, guarding those of us that were vulnerable because we were wearing our skins for the moment, while they kept a look out for anything that might try to hurt us. I hadn't expected such protection from the people of Elderthorne. Perhaps I hadn't thought highly enough of them.

"You can't think of going," someone close to us told Shae.

It was the wrong thing to say to her; I knew that instantly as Shae's gaze narrowed in the direction of the weak voice. "I do what I want," Shae challenged.

But the boy that had spoken rose from his prone position on the sandy riverbank and, his skin soaked with sweat from his shift, stepped around those that were still in the middle of their changes. He was no more than fourteen, an age I tried not to remember, but his gaze held none of the fear and anxiety that I knew mine had back then. "You're our alpha," he said as he came and sat down next to us, crowding against

Shae and touching her back. Touch was a familiar thing, especially to children, and I was glad to see that Shae accepted his affection without pushing him away.

More people began to add their voices as well, telling Shae how much they wanted her to stay, how much they needed her, how she was theirs now. I saw the trepidation and uncertainty etched into her beautiful face and leaned forward to place a gentle kiss on her mouth. "I will follow you anywhere," I told her as I pulled away. Shae nodded, and a tight smile came to her lips. "But—"

She raised her nearly black eyebrows. "There's a but?"

I smiled at her. "Sometimes there is. But, these people need an alpha. Please, consider it."

One of her shoulders lifted in a delicate shrug, and she pressed her forehead against mine. "I am glad to see my Maiki back."

I blushed and enjoyed the feeling of her hair brushing against my cheeks. "She's not, not completely, anyway. But you and your wolf gave me back my wolf. Your strength gives me strength, your hope is mine."

"My love?" Shae asked me, taking my hands from her shoulders and pressing her palms against mine.

My blush deepened. "I have always loved you, ever since I realized who you were to me, but you being here allowed me to show it again. To feel it again. For too many years this pack lived in darkness. You brought us light. Please stay with us here. Elderthorne could be a place of beauty again. The memories could be melted away with the thawing of the spring snow."

She pulled away and gave me a considering look. "You've seen it?"

I shook my head. "I have not had a dream since the last. But I believe it. And I think your wolf does too. At least that's what mine seems to be telling me. We've got a long way to go before our connection will be healed again."

Shae nodded again and released my hands as she got to her feet in the middle of the small pack. She turned in a slow circle, looking at each of them as I watched her just as everyone else in the pack did. "I am not an alpha, I have never wanted a pack, and I will not command you all. But if you are willing to put in the work to make this place a home, a real home, and to erase the horrible things that were done here, then I will stand with you."

There were happy murmurs and words of gratitude. I smiled up at my mate, my alpha, and looked forward to the future for the first time in years.

~~*

Our first test as a newly formed pack came only a few hours later as the sun began to set behind the mountains to the west of us. I found myself lounging on a rug in front of a fire surrounded by the other members of the pack. We'd spent the day going through the abandoned houses and getting rid of any of the personal items left by those that had fled with Diane. Some people thought it was cruel to burn their things. But more of them agreed with what Shae had said. About how they had sided with her and no longer mattered in the pack.

As I watched the men's things burn, I found myself agreeing with the sentiment. Though Ray had long since grown tired of using me, these men had not, and I felt my deeply buried anger coming back to me as I remembered things better left forgotten. Some of the girls cried along with me. Others screamed. And all through it Shae held my hand, an ever-silent support to show strength to my fear and hope to the constant worry that had seemed to grip my gut like a vice. The men that had used us no longer remained and after that evening their things didn't either.

With our pasts pushed to the backs of our minds, we lay together as a pack with the last of a family album in front of us. We didn't speak, and in fact most of us had barely said anything through the whole day as we went through what some of the younger werewolves were starting to refer to as the cleansing of the pack. I didn't call it anything so grand; more like taking out the trash. This was to be our fresh start. But there was still one loose end to tie up, so I guess I shouldn't have been so surprised when the first of the screams started.

Shae, the first of us to shift, bolted out of the house as soon as gray fur covered her body. My wolf wanted to run with her, to fight with her mate, to protect her, but I knew that our bond wasn't nearly strong enough for me to shift as easily as Shae was able to. It would take time, the rest of the pack had told me, but my wolf was impatient, and I was barely able to contain her as I clutched Gavin to my chest and tried to comfort those most frightened members of our pack around me. There were whispers and mumbled prayers, but as the first sounds of fighting erupted on the main street just in front of the house everyone grew quiet until the only sounds I heard were of the rapid, frightened heartbeats of the people pressed tightly against me.

I turned and faced the door, pushing Gavin behind me as my wolf continued to fight me for control. She was worried for her mate. I was worried about Shae. A shadow moved across the curtained window, the hulking body of a man in mid-shift, and I heard what sounded like it might have been a wolf in pain. That simple sound that screeched against my ears was enough to break my concentration and let my wolf out. From one heartbeat to the next, I found myself pushed back as my body crumpled to the ground.

"Maiki!" one young girl said, coming up to me and grabbing my arm. But it was already too late; I couldn't make my body respond, as my wolf had taken over my throat. She shifted as fast as she was able to, but I knew that even that bone-aching speed was too slow for my worried wolf. I could feel her frustration as a pulse through my veins while she clawed her way through my body until the only parts of me were left at the back of her mind, aching and crying out in silent pain as we fitted our broken bones back together. I knew she was in pain too as she got up on unsteady legs and took the first few shuffling steps to the door. But she'd never been this strong before either. At least, I'd never felt her like this before, and it frightened me to think of the power she wielded over me when she wanted to. She sent me comforting thoughts and I let them ease me. She meant me no harm, but her mate was in trouble. I had to understand that.

Only I did understand. I was weak where my wolf was strong, and though I'd wanted to go out there and help Shae, I hadn't been capable of it. Others began shifting behind us, and my wolf turned to give Gavin a quick nuzzle on the underside of his chin before she took off through the back door one of the children was holding open for those of us that had decided to shift. Some stayed behind, I was glad to see, and I felt that my wolf agreed as well as she turned and gave the large wolves blocking the open doorway a nod of approval.

She trotted away on light steps until she came around the side of the house. Still hidden in the shadows, my wolf watched two wolves fighting nearby but quickly lost interest when neither one of them were her mate. She kept walking, her mind on a single driven purpose, as she sought out the charcoal wolf. I could feel her worry growing as she searched for Shae's wolf until she caught a sound almost too faint for me to hear. Her ears picked it up instantly, and her head snapped in the direction of it. She was running before I'd even realized that the sound was that of someone crying.

We found Shae in an alley with blood on her hands and smeared across her mouth. A body lay at her feet, but we ignored it in favor of our mate. My wolf pressed her face against Shae's bare arm before licking at her chin. Though I was in the back of my wolf's mind and completely cut off from the outside world, she let me feel what it was like to have Shae hug her a moment later as her arms came around my wolf's shoulders and she buried her face in my wolf's neck.

I'd never seen her cry before, not even when we were kids during the worst parts of our lives. She was stronger than that, I'd thought, but as I heard her muffled sobs against the wolf's neck I wondered what could have broken that last part of herself. I didn't blame her for her tears; in fact if I were in my skin I would have been crying as well simply because she was. I asked my wolf for my body back, but she quickly denied me.

I was hurt and ready to argue with her that Shae needed me as a woman and not as a wolf right then, but then my wolf sent me images that I couldn't deny. We had to be in her form right now because she was stronger than I was. She could protect Shae, who was vulnerable. And there were children to protect. I sent her back images of Shae shifting faster than I'd ever seen anyone do before, but it was an image of Gavin alone and needing help that swayed me to her side.

She was right; we needed to be strong in case he needed us. And so I moved into the back of her mind and let the mist swirl around me as I stared out through her eyes at the woman that was my mate. Shae pulled away and wiped roughly at her cheeks before taking a deep, shuddering breath that seemed to rake through her. My wolf laid her head on Shae's shoulder, and I tried to ignore the fighting that was going on right nearby.

"I hated her, but she was still my mom," Shae whispered, her hand returning to the thick fur on my wolf's neck.

My wolf turned and looked at the body behind us, understanding just as I had. I'd hated Diane as well, and even my wolf understood why as there were plenty of times that I'd felt her rustling in the back of my mind when the woman had spoken badly of Shae. I was saddened by the death, the waste of life, but not that Shae had killed her. I remembered watching through the crack in my door when Diane had pulled Shae by her hair, kicking and screaming, down the hallway toward Ray's room. I'd sat there with my knees against my chest and the palms of my hands clasped against my ears to block out the sounds of my mate's pain. But it didn't stop all the noises from coming in, and I'd tried for nearly a decade to forget the sound of Shae's terror that first night. When Diane had come for me shortly after Shae's escape, I'd made much the same noises.

My wolf turned toward the body, and though I felt some semblance of sadness for her, the wolf had none to spare. She growled at the lifeless heap of the woman that had caused us both pain for the last ten years of our lives. I couldn't blame her for how she felt. Shae got to her feet, and my wolf pressed against her leg, steadying her when she might have gone down.

"I never thought, coming back here, that all of this would happen." She sounded distant, like she really wasn't talking to me even though her hand was on my wolf's neck. I wanted to nod; I hadn't expected it either. But now that it had happened I wasn't exactly upset by it, not in the least. There was rebuilding to be done, but I had faith that by the time the elk came back in full strength in the spring, our pack would be better than I could ever remember it being. And that was all because of Shae and what she'd managed to do for all of us. Sometimes it takes fighting and a bit of bloodshed to wash away the pain. I hadn't ever known that, but I was seeing the truth of it as we emerged from the alley to see the last of the fighting taking place.

Diane and her group were dead. I didn't have to count the bodies to know that as people started dragging them to the middle of the street. Without saying a word, two men went behind us to retrieve Diane's body and added it to the pile as well. We'd lost a few as well but not nearly the numbers that they had. I saw a teenage girl carrying Gavin and shielding his face from the carnage. I appreciated that and nodded to her. She gave me a weak smile, her face smeared with dirt as she joined the others as we all looked at the mess that had become of our little town. We were barely a mile wide, no more than twenty homes and small buildings, and could hardly even be called a town, but it had been my home. I'd been born here in Elderthorne and had known nothing else. And I could see the life under the blood and peeling paint. It needed some work, but I knew this place could be ours again.

Again I asked my wolf to let me have my body back, and this time she agreed. Though I was still left gasping and in pain as my body came back together from wherever it went when I wasn't a wolf, I felt stronger this time as I got to my feet unassisted. I took Shae's hand, grasping hers in mine and hoping she got some comfort from our connection the same as I did. "It's over," I told her.

Shae nodded and forced a watery smile. "Thanks to you all."

I quickly shook my head, knowing where the source of our strength came from. "Thanks to you. You gave these people hope and a chance to be safe.

All they needed was a chance to take it and a reason to fight. And an alpha that they could fight for."

She hugged me close, and I wrapped my arms around her as I buried my face in the softness of her slender neck. "Thank you for bringing me back here." I nodded, unable to do anything more without breaking the connection between us, which I wasn't ready to do just yet.

Someone came up behind us, and with Shae holding me close I didn't startle as I had been known to do so many times before. The fear was still there, and I had no illusions of it going away anytime soon after everything I had been through, but having her there to hold me somehow made it softer and far more manageable.

"What do you want done with the bodies?" the man asked us. I didn't want to think about it but figured that it had to be done anyway. Thankfully Shae was there to answer the question for me.

"Bury our dead and burn theirs," she told him without letting me go. It might have sounded cold and maybe even heartless of her, but I knew that was likely what everyone in the pack would have wanted anyway.

She led me away from the bodies as that gruesome work began. We took Gavin from the girl that had been holding him, and I followed her into the darkness of the surrounding forest where she sat down with her back against a wide pine tree and I found comfort on a lush bed of moss.

"Are you all right?" I asked her after a few long moments of silence stretched between us. I knew she likely wasn't after everything that had happened recently, but I couldn't simply let the silence continue on between us either. I had never been all that great with silence.

"Do you really want to stay here?" Shae asked me. Her voice sounded strained as if she couldn't quite believe the possibility of me saying yes or of even having to ask such a question.

I nodded. "I do," I told her. If she left again I would go with her, though. She was my mate, and even if I didn't love her and hadn't been in love with her for years, we were bound together, and I never wished to be away from her again.

Her face pinched and her shoulders hunched as she leaned forward and looked me squarely in the eye. "Even after everything that happened here?" she pressed me.

Smiling at her, I came forward as well. Gavin lied down between us and closed his eyes, looking nearly as exhausted as I felt. "Yes, even after all the history here, I still want to stay." I thought that she was going to argue with me, or to try to tell me all the reasons we should be going as far away from here as we could possibly get. As if I didn't already know them all by heart myself.

But instead she only simply asked me, "Why?" as if it were the most basic question in the world. And maybe it was.

I crawled toward her on my hands and knees and laid my head down on her thigh as I stretched out beside her. "Because this place, with its good and the bad, is still my home." I took a breath and pressed her hand between mine near my face. "But I won't make you stay here. If you want to leave, I will go with you. I'm sure it was hard for you to come back here this time, and if you'll be unhappy here then we can go. I won't sacrifice your happiness just because I feel like staying here."

The hard lines around Shae's face softened. "Thank you. Do you really think that we could make this place a home? A real home, and not the fake shadow of something resembling a home that it was before?" she asked me in a soft voice that reminded me of the autumn breeze as it whispered through the changing mountain leaves.

I nodded firmly. I was sure of it and felt it deeply within my heart. "I am."

She nodded as well and ran her calloused thumb gently over the back of my hand. "Then it's settled, mate. Elderthorne is our home. A few coats of paint and a few more homes demolished and it might not even look the same."

I smiled up at her and chose to ignore the way her eyes sparkled when she spoke of causing more destruction to the town. I knew her reasons, and they were shared by plenty of the people here as well. "There you go."

She gave me a wink. "Or we could just burn it all to the ground and live like wild wolves up in the hills. Killing for our dinners, bathing in the river, lying naked under the stars ..." She looked up at the moon above us as if to make a point.

She was right; we didn't live all that differently from what she was describing now. We'd all shared in the kill of a buck the night before and had cleaned ourselves in the river, and now of the three of us near this little tree, Gavin was the only one wearing pants. She was also joking. I knew this by the shining light in her eyes and the wink she had given me. And so I said, "Whatever makes you happy, Shae."

"You make me happy, mate," she quickly replied.

Heat flooded my cheeks, and I kissed her knuckles. "You make me happy too."

A chorus of howls went up around us, and though we weren't wolves, Shae and I tossed our heads back and joined in the song of our kind. We rejoiced in the music as it celebrated who we were and where we had come from. There was something magical about having a pack around me that I felt like I belonged to, one I believed in, that I felt like I could trust. I'd never had that before, and with my mate by my side and our son less than a foot away, I knew that I could believe in a brighter future together, for all of us.

about the author

Caitlin was fortunate growing up to be surrounded by family and teachers that encouraged her love of reading. She has always been a voracious reader and that love of the written word easily morphed into a passion for writing. If she isn't writing, she can usually be found studying as she works toward her counseling degree. She comes from a military family and the men and women of the armed forces are close to her heart. She also enjoys gardening, hiking, and horseback riding in the Colorado Rockies where she calls home with her wonderful fiance and their two dogs. Her belief that there is no one true path to happily ever after runs deeply through all of her stories.

CPSIA information can be obtained at www.ICGtesting.com
Printed in the USA
LVOW08s1802220414

382758LV00007B/871/P